STAR WARS®

THE CLONE WARS™

Perla
Gonzalee

2 THE LOST LEGION

Written by Tracey West   •   Story by Jake T. Forbes

Grosset & Dunlap · LucasBooks

GROSSET & DUNLAP
Published by the Penguin Group
Penguin Group (USA) Inc., 375 Hudson Street, New York, New York 10014, USA
Penguin Group (Canada), 90 Eglinton Avenue East, Suite 700, Toronto, Ontario M4P 2Y3,
Canada (a division of Pearson Penguin Canada Inc.)
Penguin Books Ltd., 80 Strand, London WC2R 0RL, England
Penguin Group Ireland, 25 St. Stephen's Green, Dublin 2, Ireland
(a division of Penguin Books Ltd.)
Penguin Group (Australia), 250 Camberwell Road, Camberwell, Victoria 3124, Australia
(a division of Pearson Australia Group Pty. Ltd.)
Penguin Books India Pvt. Ltd., 11 Community Centre, Panchsheel Park,
New Delhi—110 017, India
Penguin Group (NZ), 67 Apollo Drive, Rosedale, North Shore 0632,
New Zealand (a division of Pearson New Zealand Ltd.)
Penguin Books (South Africa) (Pty.) Ltd., 24 Sturdee Avenue,
Rosebank, Johannesburg 2196, South Africa

Penguin Books Ltd., Registered Offices:
80 Strand, London WC2R 0RL, England

This book is published in partnership with LucasBooks, a division of Lucasfilm Ltd.
Copyright © 2009 Lucasfilm Ltd. & ® or ™ where indicated. All Rights Reserved. Used Under
Authorization. Published by Grosset & Dunlap, a division of Penguin Young Readers Group,
345 Hudson Street, New York, New York 10014. GROSSET & DUNLAP is a trademark
of Penguin Group (USA) Inc. Printed in the U.S.A.

Library of Congress Control Number: 2008053542

ISBN 978-0-448-45036-0   10 9 8 7 6 5 4 3 2

"All Level 13 clones please report to Training Room 27-A."

You're in the middle of eating your morning meal, a flavorless block of proteins and carbohydrates designed to deliver maximum nutrition to your body. At the sound of the voice on the speaker, you immediately put down your fork. Two hundred forks clatter on plates at the same time as every Level 13 clone responds to the command.

It's automatic. You've learned to respond to the voice of your keepers ever since the day you were created. Unlike other beings in the galaxy, you weren't born like a Corellian or even a duracrete slug. You weren't built in a factory like a droid.

You're a clone, created in a laboratory on the planet Kamino. You are technically ten years old, but thanks to Kaminoan technology, clones mature twice as fast as other humanoids. You look like you're twenty years old. Because your DNA all comes from the same source, you and every other clone look pretty much the same. You're tall and muscular, with black hair and brown eyes. You all wear identical orange jumpsuits.

Right now, the only thing that separates you from

the other clones in your training group is the serial number on the back of your neck. You don't exactly have friends, but you have developed a bond with the clones who sit near you during meals and learning time. During the few moments a day when you have time to talk, you call each other by the last two digits of your serial number. You've been called 18 for as long as you can remember.

You line up with the other clones and march down a long tube with clear walls to the training room. The tubes connect all of the buildings in Tipoca City. The shining metal-and-glass buildings are the only home you've ever known. You've never once been outside these walls.

As you head to the training room, a strange feeling comes over you. You think it might be excitement—something you've never really felt before. You know that Level 13 is the last level of training you will complete. The last ten years have been leading up to this moment: You are about to become a fighting member of the clone army. Finally, you'll be able to leave Kamino and explore the universe.

You glance outside at the swirling waters that surround Tipoca City—an endless sea of blue-black, choppy waves. In your studies, you have learned about every known planet in the universe. You have seen pictures of snow, rocks, and green grass, but the pictures are never enough. You wonder how cold snow is, what grass feels like under your feet . . .

"Hey, Eighteen, step it up!" a clone behind you says. You realize you were lost in thought and pick up your pace.

You file into the training room with the other clones and take a seat at your learning station. You reach for your learning helmet.

"No helmets will be necessary today."

You pause at the voice of your teacher, Yan So. Your teacher is a Kaminoan, the only other life-form you have seen in person. Like all Kaminoans, Yan So is impossibly tall and thin with a very long neck. Large eyes are the biggest feature on his smooth, white head.

"Your training is complete," Yan So announces. "Today you will take a test—perhaps the most important test of your life. The results of the test will determine which role you will take when you are assigned to a fighting squad."

That feeling of excitement surges through you again. You're going to be assigned to a squad! You wonder who your commander will be. You have read about all of the major battles in the Republic's war against the Separatist Alliance. Jedi generals lead squads of clone soldiers into battle. You've read a lot about Commander Cody. He's been in some of the biggest battles in the war. It would be great to be assigned to him, but you doubt you'll be so lucky on your first assignment.

Before your test begins, another Kaminoan enters the room. She nods to Yan So.

"Ah, Taun We," the teacher says. "I understand you have a special announcement."

You know that Taun We is the project coordinator for the clone army, but you've never seen her. Her skin is a pale blue-gray, and her gray skirt covers her long legs. You guess if Taun We is here, something important is about to happen.

You are right. "The clone army needs a squad for a very important mission led by Commander Vargus," she announces. "Only the best clone troopers will be selected. I have reviewed your training records and will be selecting seven of you for the mission."

"But first, the test," Yan So says. "Please turn on your monitors."

You press a button and the screen in front of you lights up. You take a deep breath. Going on a special mission right out of Kamino would be incredible. You hope Taun We selects you—but you know the odds are against you.

You look at the screen and begin to answer the questions.

1. If you could carry only one tool on a mission, which would it be?

a. a map of your surroundings
(1 point)

b. a thermal detonator
(2 points)

c. a portable FX-3 medical droid
(3 points)

d. a helmet with a built-in comlink antenna
(4 points)

2. The most valuable skill a clone soldier can have is the ability to:

a. lead
(4 points)

b. heal injured soldiers
(3 points)

c. destroy
(2 points)

d. remain undetected in enemy territory
(1 point)

3. You and your squad are attacked by three super battle droids. It's a surprise attack, and two clones go down. Your first instinct is to:

a. run to the injured soldiers and bring them to safety
(3 points)

b. search for the droid's command center to prevent another attack
(1 point)

c. lead the squad to cover and attack the droids from a safe vantage point
(4 points)

d. fire at the droids with a plasma detonator
(2 points)

4. Which of these would you rather examine?

a. a blueprint of an enemy command center
(2 points)

b. the skeleton of a wampa beast
(3 points)

c. the enemy's battle formation
(4 points)

d. the inner circuitry of a Mustafarian blaster
(1 point)

5. Which of these words or phrases best describes you?

a. fearless
   (1 point)

b. quick-thinking
   (4 points)

c. intelligent
   (3 points)

d. curious
   (2 points)

6. What kind of planet would you like to visit on your first assignment?

a. a planet in the middle of a war
   (4 points)

b. a planet holding an intergalactic science library
   (3 points)

c. a completely deserted planet
   (1 point)

d. a planet filled with crowded, complex cities
   (2 points)

7. What is your preferred method of physical exercise?

a. a course of unpredictable obstacles
(1 point)

b. a timed maze
(2 points)

c. a brisk hike with the rest of your squad
(4 points)

d. a series of exercises designed specifically
to enhance your physical performance
(3 points)

8. What is your greatest physical talent?

a. strength
(4 points)

b. speed
(1 point)

c. agility
(2 points)

d. endurance
(3 points)

9. You are on a mission, and a laser blast comes out of nowhere, striking your squad leader. What is the first thing you do?

a. Rush to his side to tend to his injuries.
(3 points)

b. Take control of the squad yourself.
A squad needs a leader.
(4 points)

c. Storm the enemy attackers before they take down any more members of your squad.
(1 point)

d. Scan the area to see where the attack came from.
(2 points)

10. What do you hope you will be doing five years from today?

a. blowing up battle droids
(1 point)

b. planning surprise attacks with my commander
(2 points)

c. getting an award for saving the lives of my squad members
(3 points)

d. commanding a squad of my own
(4 points)

You are surprised by the test. Every other test you've taken is about facts and figures you've memorized. But this test is about *you* and how *you* think. You have no idea how well you did, or what your results will be.

Taun We said this would be the most important test of your life. You don't want to blow it. Just to be sure, you look over your answers one last time before pressing the enter button. Then you submit your answers and hope for the best.

Add up your score. Then follow the instructions to learn your assignment.

If you scored 10-14 points, turn to page 32.
If you scored 15-24 points, turn to page 57.
If you scored 25-34 points, turn to page 80.
If you scored 35-40 points, turn to page 101.

"This will just take a minute," you tell Falco. You know he won't be happy with your decision. He might outrank you, but you have the final say on all medical decisions. You can't just leave the Talid to freeze in the snow.

You kneel down to tend to the Talid. His face is covered with layers of scarves.

"Name's Eighteen," you tell him. "Let me take a look at your leg."

"Thank you," the Talid says gruffly.

You take the pack off of your back and slowly push the Talid's fur robes aside. Both legs are covered in coarse, white hair. His right shin is swollen and purple.

Probably a fracture, you guess. You gently feel the injury and the Talid winces. As far as you can tell, the bone isn't broken clean through. It's probably a minor fracture.

There's only so much you can do with your field kit. You apply an airsplint to the leg to stabilize it. Then you help the Talid to his feet.

"Is there a doctor back in your village?" you ask.

The Talid nods.

"You might need a cast. But this should get you back home," you say.

"Thank you, Eighteen." The Talid sighs. "I am Gen-Goma, and I am in your debt. I cannot return to my village until I repay you."

Gen-Goma doesn't sound too happy about offering to help you. You suspect it's some kind of rule in his culture.

"We're looking for five thousand clone troopers," Falco says. "Any idea where they are?"

"Yes, there were many, many troopers. Many, many droids," Gen-Goma says. "There was fighting. Then a big explosion. The sky opened up. Then they were all gone."

"They all blew up?" you ask.

Gen-Goma shakes his head. "No, no. Gone. Just gone. I can take you there. You will see."

He starts to limp down the trail. You know you need the Talid's help, but you don't know if he'll make it on that leg. You have an idea.

"Where did your Podracer crash?" you ask.

"Just around that bend there," Gen-Goma says, pointing.

You turn to Falco. "I'll be right back."

You run to the abandoned Podracer. It's beyond repair, but you are able to make a crude sled from a metal wing panel and some wiring. You bring the sled back to Gen-Goma and Falco.

"Here," you say. "I'll pull you."

Falco shakes his head. "Crazy rookie," he mutters. But Gen-Goma seems grateful for the transport.

After a few meters you wonder if Falco is right. The Talid is a lot heavier than he looks. But you plod on without complaining. You don't want Falco to think you can't hack it.

From the sled, Gen-Goma directs you over a hill and down into a steep valley. Then it's over another hill and you see it—the Confederacy outpost. Several crudely made metal and wood buildings are scattered across the snow. There are long barracks where their soldiers would be stationed. But the buildings look deserted.

"My village is not far from here," Gen-Goma says. You can tell that he can't wait to get away from here.

"Thanks for your help," you say. "Good luck with that leg."

Gen-Goma limps off, and you and Falco descend into the compound. Your first order of business is to check out each of the buildings and make sure they're empty. The first two are clear—but in the third one, you find something.

It's another humanoid—at least you think it is. The tall figure has a metal armored mask over his face and armored plates over his thick robes. The greenish yellow skin behind the mask is thick and bumpy. The figure is lying on a table. You lean over and hear shallow, sharp breathing.

"That's a Skakoan," Falco says. "Met one once before. They never take off their armor. Pretty creepy, if you ask me."

You don't remember learning about Skakoans on Kamino. How are you supposed to fix something if you don't know how it works inside?

Then you remember your portable FX-3 medical droid. Maybe there's something in its data banks to help you.

You remove the droid from your pouch and place it on the table. It rolls along the length of the Skakoan's body, scanning it.

"Sensing failure of the primary filtration organ," the droid reports.

"Report location," you say.

"Unable to determine," the droid replies.

Looks like you're going to have to figure this out yourself. You pry open the Skakoan's armor to reveal more thick, greenish yellow skin. You press your ear to his abdomen. In the lower-left quadrant you can hear a thumping sound to indicate a heart or other blood-pumping organ. There's no sign of swelling or injury on the skin.

You think. A filtration organ usually cleans toxins

from the body. A bacta injection might be just the thing to revive the Skakoan.

But if the filtration organ is damaged, more drastic measures might be necessary. You glance at your scalpel. Should you open up the Skakoan and see what's inside?

If you decide to operate, turn to page 99.
If you decide to go with the bacta injection, turn to page 148.

You have to admit that the troopers have a point. Taking the Podracers would save a lot of time. Besides, you've always wanted to try Podracing, too.

"Let's see if we can get the Podracers started," you say.

Since the ridge is at the top of the canyon, it's easy for you to scale down. You and 23 head for one of the racers. You've always thought Podracers were strange-looking, and this one is no exception. There's a small cockpit stuffed with levers and buttons. Two long rods extend from the back of the cockpit, and at the end of each one is a massive, tunnel-shaped turbine engine. It doesn't look like the vehicle should be able to get off of the ground, but you've seen images of them racing at dizzying speeds.

This one had a bold orange and yellow paint job once, but the paint is faded and peeled. Still, it looks more exciting than anything you've ever tested on Kamino. You can't wait to find out what it feels like to pilot one.

The cockpit of your Podracer must have been designed for a Hutt pilot, because there's room for both you and 23 to fit side by side on the seat. You glance over at the other Podracer and see that Bruiser's in the cockpit, but 35 can't fit. He's perched behind the cockpit seat.

You think that looks dangerous, but before you can say anything, Bruiser's Podracer roars to life. Flames shoot out of the engines, nearly hitting you. Bruiser lets out a whoop as the Podracer lifts off of the ground.

You study the controls for a moment and then start the engines. The sound is deafening. You can feel the Podracer rise underneath you.

"Straight across the canyon," you tell Bruiser via comlink.

"Woo hoo!" is Bruiser's reply. "Let's take these babies for a spin!"

Bruiser takes off, zipping along the Podracer track. He's not listening to you at all! You're annoyed. You press the propulsion forward and zoom after him.

Bruiser's going fast, and 35 is getting tossed from side to side. You watch in horror as he loses his grip on the seat. He grabs onto one of the engine rods.

"Hang on, Thirty-Five. Coming to get you," you say.

You race up alongside Bruiser, hoping to grab 35. But Bruiser can't keep the racer stable. He slams into you.

You both go toppling down into the canyon. It's a long way down. You slam into the ice, and then begin to slide across the canyon floor. There's a nasty icy crevice in the floor of the canyon, and both Podracers slide right into it. You brace yourself for another crash.

The four of you are battered, but not seriously hurt. There's only one problem. The sides of the crevice are icy and steep. Bruiser makes an effort to scale up the sides, but he just slides back down. Without the proper tools, climbing up the ice is impossible. There's no way out.

"We can contact Falco," you say. "Maybe he can figure out a way to get us out of here."

You're not sure what Falco can do—but right now, he's your only hope.

THE END

You feel bad for the Talid—but Falco is an ARF, after all. He's been in battle before, and you're just a rookie. You decide to listen to him and stick to the mission.

You walk around the injured Talid without saying a word. Then you continue down the trail. Snow begins to fall, lightly at first, and then heavier. A cold wind whips up around you.

Now the snow is falling in sheets. You can see only a few steps ahead of you. Falco doesn't seem bothered by it.

"Should we go back to the ship?" you ask.

"We've made it this far," Falco says. "Might as well keep going. I think we're getting closer to the Confederacy outpost."

You continue, but you are starting to feel the cold even though your insulated armor is designed to keep you warm in freezing temperatures. You can't help thinking of the Talid back on the trail. You know he probably won't survive long in the storm.

After what seems like hours, you reach the mountains that you saw back when you started. The trail forks off in two directions. One leads up to a path that seems to lead around one of the mountains. The other leads to a deep, frozen gorge.

"I've lost the trail," Falco admits. "This blizzard's making it impossible to track anything."

"Do you think the outpost is on the other side of that mountain?" you ask.

"Could be," Falco replies. "Or it could be through that gorge."

If you and Falco take the path around the mountain, turn to page 42.

If you and Falco travel through the gorge, turn to page 141.

Part of being a leader is knowing your strengths and weaknesses. You're not sure if you've got what it takes yet to take down a droid comm station.

Besides, you really want to go into battle with Commander Cody.

"I'll help Cody search for the general," you say.

"Excellent," Obi-Wan Kenobi replies. "We'll have the comm station down as quickly as possible."

Obi-Wan leads Bruiser and Falco down the side of the cliff. Cody takes a minute to scan the battle area with his long-distance binoculars.

"I can see the general's unit there on the front line," he says, pointing. "Let's go."

Cody unclips his laser rifle and points it forward as he scrambles down the cliffside. You only have your blaster on you, but you're loaded and ready to go. Dusty earth kicks up under your feet as you go.

When you get to the edge of the battle, you're not sure how you and Cody are going to make it all the way to General Bandis. But Cody doesn't hesitate. He fearlessly plows through the line of droids.

The droids immediately turn on you both. But Cody is faster.

Zap! Zap! Zap! He blasts three battle droids in a

row before they can even aim their blasters. The droids clatter to the ground.

The droids are converging on you now, but your training kicks in. You put your back to Cody and handle the droids on the other side.

It's a good system. You quickly reach General Bandis. He's wearing a tunic like Obi-Wan Kenobi's, but he's clearly from a different planet. He's got four small horns growing from his forehead and dark brown skin.

General Bandis is surprised to see Cody—and equally surprised to learn that General Kenobi is on the strange planet.

Cody outlines the rescue plan.

"Once the comm station is down, it should be easy to push the droids back," Cody says. "We need to make sure the legion is held in one location. Then General Kenobi will activate the device to get us all back to Ando Prime."

And that's exactly what happens. True to his word, Obi-Wan Kenobi quickly takes out the comm station. The confused droids erupt into chaos. They're easily defeated, and soon the lost legion is back on Ando Prime.

Obi-Wan Kenobi and Cody go back to Excelsior Company's ship with you to touch base with Commander Vargus.

"You've got a good squad," Cody says. "I've recommended to General Kenobi that your sergeant here gets promoted to lieutenant for his good work."

"That's a fine idea," General Kenobi agrees.

Lieutenant! You're rising through the ranks really fast. That's even better than getting a cool nickname.

But you hope it won't be long before you get one of those, too.

THE END

"Let's move left," Falco says.

You cautiously travel around the perimeter. There's no break in the line of tanks. But Falco notices something. A low-hanging cliff overlooks the camp. He devises a plan.

"I'll scale the cliff, then jump down on top of that tank there," he says. "If I hit the engine directly with my blaster rifle I can take it down. Then, Eighteen, you can run in and blow up that machine. The hard part will be getting back out. Splice and Forty-Four will give you cover."

"Sounds like a plan," you say. "Let's do it."

You, Splice, and 44 take cover behind a boulder and wait for Falco to make his move. It doesn't take long. You hear a loud blast, and then the tank in front of you topples over onto its side. Falco jumps down from the top.

Ranks of droids scramble to the tank. The diversion is just what you need. You run into the center of camp. You hurl one, two, then three pulse grenades at your target.

Boom! Boom! Boom! The explosions rock the camp.

You race back to your squad. Falco, Splice, and 44

are firing like crazy all around you, and you turn your head to see that you're being chased by battle droids. Falco shoots the droid tank next to him with his rifle and the tank topples over, taking down a line of droids with it.

It gives you enough time to get away and head back to the Republic base. General Bandis is thrilled to know the weapon is destroyed. He quickly gathers the legion in an area one kilometer away from the droid army. Falco activates the device Vylagos gave him, and before you know it you're all back on Ando Prime.

The troopers of the 313th Legion are all a little confused. General Bandis has a mess to sort out, but his spirits are high.

"Your men saved my legion," he tells Commander Vargus. "I will inform the Jedi Council that commendations are in store for all of you."

You feel great. It's your first mission ever as a clone trooper, and you're getting a commendation from the Jedi Council. Things don't get much better than that!

THE END

"I'll tell you what we're going to do," you say. "We're going after Falco."

"But—" 44 begins.

"But nothing," you say. "We were sent out here with Falco, and we're not going back without him. If something happened to him, then he needs our help."

The two troopers don't argue. You march off into the mountain pass.

Snow-covered slopes rise up on either side of you. You're protected from the wind now, and you feel a little bit warmer under your armor. It makes you feel stronger, and you start to feel good about your choice. You're going to find Falco, and Commander Vargus will be impressed that you took decisive action on your own.

57 keeps pace with you, but 44 lags behind. You're not sure if it's because he's afraid, or just plain slow. You're beginning to think that "Slug" is a good name for your squad member. It's tempting to call him that, but you don't want to discourage him. Just hours ago you two were in the same situation, two newly trained clones eager to start your first mission. You should stick together.

You stop and turn around. "Hey, Forty-Four. Catch up!" you say.

44 runs up to you. Tiny, frosty clouds form from his breath as he runs.

"Keep pace," you say. "I don't want to lose another man. We still have to find Falco."

"How will we know where to look for him?" 44 asks.

"For now we can assume he took the path through to the other side of the mountain," you say. "Once we get there, we'll look for tracks in the snow."

"You mean tracks like those?" 57 asks.

He points down to the snow in front of you, and you see the snow-covered ground is littered with prints. The pass must be a well-traveled trail for the native inhabitants of the planet. You read about them on the trip to Ando Prime.

They're primitive nomads with isolated settlements scattered across the planet. They've got thick, hairy skin that protects them from the cold. Armor and thick fur robes also help save them from Ando Prime's harsh climate. When humanoids began to explore Ando Prime, they found the Talid to be willing traders. They're big junk collectors, known for making useful objects out of any scrap they find.

"The Talid people of Ando Prime are friendly," you tell your squad. "No danger."

"No," 57 says. "I mean these tracks."

He points to a line of large, three-toed tracks in the snow. Whatever creature left them must be huge.

"Those are some big feet," 44 says nervously.

You search your memory. The Talid get around on big reptile-like creatures called tantas—similar to the tauntauns on Hoth, another icy planet. They're big and strong, but are they dangerous? You can't seem to remember.

Then it hits you.

"They're herbivores," you say. "Plant eaters. The Talid tame them and ride them. Nothing to worry about."

44 doesn't seem convinced. "Really big," he mutters.

But there are no more questions. You plod on, feeling proud of yourself. You answered your men's questions confidently. You're glad you took the time to study Ando Prime on the trip.

Bam!

A pile of snow explodes beside you. You stop.

"What was that?" 44 asks.

Bam! Bam!

It takes a second to register—you're being fired at! You scan the mountainside.

Bam! Bam! Bam!

57 raises his blaster. "Where are they coming from?"

You hate to admit it, but you're not sure. You don't know what's happening. Are droids attacking you? Could it be the Talid?

Whatever you do, you have to act fast. You see a shallow cave in the wall of the mountain up ahead. It might make good cover—or it could leave you trapped.

If you lead your men to higher ground, turn to page 121.

If you seek cover inside the cave, turn to page 128.

You don't have to wait long. Yan So walks back into the room soon after the test is complete.

"The following trainees must report immediately to the transport bay," he begins. He starts to read out the serial numbers. You hold your breath. The first five numbers aren't yours. But the last—

"—Eighteen," Yan So says, finishing the long list. It's you!

You stand up and march out of the training room. The other five selected clones all wear blank faces. You wonder if they're just as excited inside as you are.

You travel down several corridors until you reach the large, metal doors of the transport bay. You enter as the doors slide open.

Two clones in white body armor are loading a large gunship. It has a deep hull and two wings that are angled downward and topped with huge laser cannons. A clone commander is standing in front of the ship. You know he's a commander because of the rank badge on his chest plate. He's not wearing his helmet, and you see that his head is completely bald. He has a scar across the bridge of his nose.

You and the five other clones stop and stare, not sure what to do. The commander shakes his head.

"Rookies. Just great," he says as though you're not even there. "Guess every other trooper is out there somewhere doing the Republic's dirty work."

He marches up to the line of rookie troopers. "Which one of you is Eighteen?"

"I am, sir," you reply.

He looks you in the eyes. "Taun We's assigned you to recon for this mission. Think you can handle it?"

Reconnaissance. It's a dangerous position—you'll be sent out ahead of the squad to gather intelligence in enemy territory. You always excelled at recon during learning simulations. You've never done it for real—but you're not about to back out now.

"Yes, sir," you reply.

The commander nods, satisfied. "Listen up," he says. "I'm Commander Vargus. Welcome to Excelsior Company. Nobody makes a move unless I say so, understand?"

"Yes, sir!" all six of you reply. You are really excited now. You've been assigned to Commander Vargus. This must be the special mission Taun We was talking about.

"Now board the ship and get suited up," Vargus says. "I'll brief you on the mission in ten minutes."

You head up the loading ramp into the gunship. For the last ten years, you've been training for this very moment. You know exactly what to expect. You head directly to the troopers' quarters where you find a locker already stamped with your serial number. You open it up and find your body armor inside.

The body armor is made up of twenty separate white plates and fits you like a glove. You put it on and then strap your utility belt around your waist. Different compartments in the belt hold magazines for your DC-15 blaster, survival gear, and other assault equipment. You pick up your helmet and carry it under your arm. Then you report to the bridge.

Commander Vargus is there with the two clones you saw earlier. He nods to one of them, a clone with a serious expression on his face.

"This is Splice, your medic," Vargus says. "Nobody patches up a body better than Splice."

The medic's expression doesn't change. Then Vargus nods to the clone next to him. His brown hair has been dyed blue. It's cut short, and he's shaved arrows on the left and right sides of his head.

"This is Dom," Vargus said. "He's our demolitions man."

Dom grins. "I like to blow things up."

Vargus walks to the command console and presses a button. A map appears on a screen behind the console. The map zeroes in on a white planet that appears to be covered with ice and snow.

"This is Ando Prime," Vargus tells you. "Twenty-four hours ago, the 313th Legion, led by Jedi General Po Bandis, launched an attack on a Confederacy outpost there. It was a routine operation. But sometime during the attack, the entire legion disappeared."

"But that's thousands of troopers," you say.

"What do you mean, disappeared?" Dom asked. "How do we know they weren't vaporized by a pulse bomb or something?"

"There are no readings to indicate that kind of explosion," Vargus explained. "And there were no emergency transmissions made. One second they were there, and then they weren't."

"And what are we supposed to do?" Dom asked.

"We're going to find them," Commander Vargus said flatly.

Dom laughed. "Now I know why we've got so many rookies on board. Might as well call us the Expendables."

For the first time in your life, you feel afraid. You thought being chosen for this mission was an honor. Now you're not so sure.

You're not angry, because you just weren't trained that way. The Kaminoans were very specific when they designed you. The urge to obey runs through your DNA. It's all you know. If you disappear on Ando Prime, just like the others, the Kaminoans will just make more troopers to replace you. That's what it means to be a clone.

But a small part of you is pushing through the obedience.

I'll survive this mission, that voice inside you says. Nobody's going to replace me.

Vargus orders one of the rookies, 57, to pilot the ship. You march back to the troopers' quarters where you sit on a bench with the other rookies. You realize that clone trooper armor may be good in a battle situation, but it's not very comfortable to sit in.

The gunship leaves Kamino and then launches into hyperspace. Like most clones, your squadmates aren't big talkers. So you're relieved when Commander Vargus orders you back to the bridge.

He's standing over a holographic console projecting a 3-D map of Ando Prime.

"Since you're doing recon, you need to know where we're heading," Vargus says. He hands you a small holoprojector. "All the data you need is in here. Study it."

"Yes, sir," you reply, and head back to quarters. You spend the rest of the journey exploring the terrain of Ando Prime on the holoprojector. The snow-covered planet is dotted with mountains, glaciers, frozen rivers, and ice sheets. Towns and even some small cities are scattered across the landscape, all of them centered around underground mining centers.

You can see from the data that the gunship is headed to a mountainous region on the planet. It's where General Bandis was when he sent his last recorded transmission. The area looks like it's in the middle of nowhere. You wonder how a legion of thousands of clone troopers could have simply disappeared there.

Finally, the ship lands. It's time for action. You put on your helmet and grab your blaster.

Since you're recon, you'll be the first to explore the area. Commander Vargus sends 57 along with you.

"There's a gorge two hundred meters west of here," Vargus explains. "It's the most likely location for a droid base I can find on the map. Check it out. If you see anything besides ice and snow, report back."

You nod, and then you and 57 head out onto the frozen planet. At first sight, Ando Prime reminds you of Tipoca City—nothing but white as far as you can see. Then a cold wind blows up a swell of snow beside you, and it hits you.

You're not on Kamino anymore.

57 walks by your side, his blaster ready to fire. You're glad for the backup. You'd hate to be off guard while you're checking your holomap. Your body armor

manages to keep you fairly warm as you trek west across the snowy plain.

You attach the map to your belt and keep walking, eyes open for any sign of the lost legion. Then you stop. The wind is whipping up the snow at your feet, but even through the white mist you can clearly see tracks in the snow. They could be footprints. You motion to 57.

"Let's find some cover," you say. Those tracks could belong to the legion, or they could belong to the Separatists. You need to be careful.

The ground is dotted with snow-covered boulders, so you make your way from rock to rock, ducking as you run. You soon see that your instinct was right. Up ahead is a small squad of droids!

Their leader is a cyborg wearing a red and dark gray cape. You recognize him right away. It's General Grievous, one of the most powerful leaders in the Separatist army. You hold back a gasp.

Grievous is talking on a holoprojector to a man in a black hooded cloak.

"There is no sign of our army, Count Dooku," Grievous is saying. "It is as though they vanished into thin air."

"Impossible!" the hooded figure boomed. "Find them, General. We cannot afford a loss this great."

Count Dooku's image fades. General Grievous

mutters something and then heads on toward the gorge.

"What do we do now?" 57 whispers.

If you decide to follow the droid squad so you don't lose their trail, turn to page 64.

If you contact Commander Vargus before taking action, turn to page 123.

It's your first chance to blow something up, and
you decide to go big. You activate six thermal
detonators and place them in front of the fallen
boulders.

Then you run.

BOOM!

The whole tunnel shakes around you. There's
a whoosh of hot air as the force of the explosion
slams into you, sending you flying forward. You land
facedown in the dirt.

"It's a collapse!" you hear Vargus yell. You
scramble to your feet as the walls of the service tunnel
start to cave in around you.

The blast was too big, you realize, and you
suddenly remember your training. You've got to be
extra careful setting explosions inside a tunnel.

But it's too late now.

You reach the squad. The air is thick with dust.
Several troopers are buried under the rubble. The
tunnel walls have caved in behind them, blocking the
way to the tunnel entrance.

"Move, trooper," Vargus orders. "We've got to get
those men free."

You rush to help Falco, who's scrambling to lift up

a small pile of rocks pinning down one of the troopers. He shakes his head when he sees you.

"Rookie," he says.

You don't answer, and work as hard as you can. Nobody is seriously hurt, and you're able to free them all from the rubble. That's the good news.

The bad news is pretty bad. Thanks to you, the tunnel walls have collapsed. There's no way in or out.

Excelsior Company is trapped!

THE END

"Let's try the mountain," Falco says.

You nod and follow him up the sloping trail. As the path takes you up the mountain, you look down to see the frozen land below. For a second, it makes you a little bit dizzy. You've been in all kinds of environments in training simulations before, but they didn't really prepare you for the real thing.

A wicked wind whips across the mountain, and you nearly lose your footing. Heart pounding, you steady yourself and keep going.

It seems pretty dangerous, trekking across a mountain in a blizzard. But you know ARFs are tough. You're not going to complain, either. If you ever make it back to the ship, you hope Falco will put in a good word about you with Commander Vargus.

Suddenly, there's a sound above you like the roar of some strange beast. You look up to see a huge wave of snow sliding down the mountain at superspeed.

"Avalanche!" Falco yells.

You quickly search your mind—what are you supposed to do in an avalanche? But all you can think to do is run. You can't run away from it, so you race back down the path.

It's no use. The snow pours over you like a tidal

wave, knocking you facedown onto the path. You struggle to stand as the heavy snow piles on top of you. You try not to panic. Your suit will provide you with oxygen if you need it. If you stay calm, you can get out of this.

The thunderous sound of the avalanche stops, and you realize your head is sticking above the piled snow. But snow is packed tightly around your body, and you can't move your arms or legs.

You scan the path. There's no sign of Falco.

"Falco!" you yell.

There's no answer.

You don't have many options. You can try to dig your way out of the snow, but that might take a while. If you're lucky, Vargus will send out a search party to find you and Falco.

You just hope your suit will keep you warm enough until they get there. Otherwise, your fate will be the same as that injured Talid you left on the path.

THE END

The EMF generator is located on the ground a few meters behind the machine. You run to it and take a look.

It's a black box about five meters long and two meters wide. Buttons on the top flash green to show that the device is working. You know from your training that there's no off switch—it's designed for protection. The only way to turn it off is to destroy it, as far as you can remember.

You reach for a thermal detonator, but something clicks. There's another way to deactivate the generator. Some of the charges in your bag emit electronic pulses that scramble all frequencies in a two-hundred-meter radius. That's exactly what you need.

You set the electronic charge and step back. A high-pitched sound fills the air as the pulse explodes next to the generator. The machine sizzles, and the green lights flicker and finally turn off. The glowing energy shield around the machine vanishes.

"That's right!" you say, pumping a fist in the air. You've been given three tasks so far, and you've aced each one of them.

"Nice job, Eighteen," Vargus says. You notice that he isn't calling you "rookie" anymore. "Now let's take a look at this thing."

"I would not get too close if I were you."

You turn at the sound of a strange voice. It belongs to a tall figure wearing silver armored plates over his long robes. A metal plate protects the front of his face. Behind the mask, you see thick, bumpy skin that's a strange yellow green color.

"Guessed you missed one, Falco," Vargus says.

The ARF shrugs. "Not sure how that happened."

Vargus nods, and the rest of the squad members surround the stranger, blasters raised.

"I can assure you I mean you no harm," the stranger says. "I am Vylagos, an engineer from the planet Skako. This machine is my invention."

"So you're working with the Separatists?" Vargus asks suspiciously.

"Working *for* the Separatists is more correct," Vylagos responds. "I have no loyalty to either side in this ridiculous war. And I can prove it to you. I assume you are here to locate your lost Republic legion. I can tell you how to find them."

"I'm listening," Vargus says.

"The Separatists hired me to create a hyperspace warping device capable of transporting large droid troops across the galaxy," Vylagos explains. "I have been working on this base for months under the protection of General Terrus. Then your Republic legion attacked unexpectedly, and the device was accidentally activated. Both the legion and General Terrus's droid army were transported somewhere."

"Where?" Vargus asks.

Vylagos shakes his head. "I am not completely certain. I have been trying to repair the machine so I can bring them back. I will not get paid if General Terrus is not returned."

Vargus studies the scientist carefully. "How soon can you fix it?"

"I need supplies," Vylagos answers. "I can purchase the equipment I need from a Talid trading post over the mountain. If you let me go, I will go to the trading post now and return by morning."

"I have a better idea," Vargus says. "You give me a list, and I'll send some of my men to get what you need. I think it's a good idea to keep an eye on you."

"As you wish," Vylagos says stiffly. You sense he's not too pleased with the new arrangement.

"Okay," Vargus says. "Falco, take Eighteen and Five-Seven with you."

Turn to page 74.

"You know where the lost legion is?" you repeat.

Obi-Wan Kenobi nods. "Cody and I finished up a skirmish on a nearby planet, so we came to Ando Prime yesterday to investigate," he says. His voice is as smooth as a Kaminoan protein shake. You've never seen a Jedi before, and there's something about him you can't quite put your finger on. It's like he's got a different energy than everyone else in the room.

You try to concentrate as General Kenobi continues.

"We detected a massive hyperspace rift in this outpost and traced it to a machine. It appears the machine was designed to warp large amounts of troops across the galaxy. We're guessing the Separatists engineered it to launch a surprise attack on someplace heavily guarded, such as Coruscant."

You see how that could work. But you still have questions.

"So why did the legion get caught in the warp? And where did they go?"

"Our best guess is that the machine was accidentally activated when General Bandis launched the attack on the base," General Kenobi replies. "We're not sure where they are, but we know the location is beyond the Outer Rim."

"So how do we get them back?" you ask.

"I spent the night analyzing the equipment," General Kenobi says. "There's a small homing device that must be transported to wherever the legion is. If we can get the legion concentrated to a one kilometer radius, we can bring them back here."

Commander Cody stands up. "The general and I are going through the warp," he says. "We could use a squad to go with us."

You look at Falco and Bruiser. "What do you say?" you ask. "We can leave Twenty-Three and Thirty-Five here to guard the machine."

"I can do recon anywhere," Falco says confidently. "Whether it's across a canyon or across the universe."

"Will I get to blow stuff up?" Bruiser asks.

Cody shrugs. "Probably."

Bruiser grins. "What are we waiting for?"

Obi-Wan Kenobi leads you to the machine. You put on your helmet as he presses some buttons on the console.

You're not sure what to expect, and it doesn't occur to you to be afraid until a loud, strange hum fills the air. You feel an impossible pressure on your body and think, What if this doesn't work?

Thankfully, the feeling doesn't last. Things calm

down, and you realize you're not on Ando Prime anymore. For one thing, there's no snow. The ground at your feet is reddish brown. You scan the area and see a barren landscape dotted with rocks.

You take a step forward, and you're feeling a little shaky. It must be the effects of the transporter. You stop and take a deep breath.

"Well, that was weird," Bruiser says next to you. "Hey look, we're on top of a cliff. Good thing we didn't land a few meters south."

Obi-Wan Kenobi strides to the edge and looks down. "I think I've found them," he says.

You follow him and see that a full-scale battle is being waged in the valley below. Five thousand clones and what may be just as many droids are exchanging round after round of laser blasts.

"There's no way we'll get the legion home with this going on," Obi-Wan Kenobi says. "We must find General Bandis."

Commander Cody points to a spot in the valley. "That looks like a droid comm station there, sir," he says. "If we take that down, we can do some quick damage to the droid army."

"Then it's a good thing we have a squad with us," General Kenobi says. "Sergeant, I understand this is your first mission. Are you up to leading your men in an attack on the comm station? If you prefer, I can lead the attack, and you can accompany Commander Cody into battle to locate the general."

You're not sure what to say. Fighting side by side with Commander Cody would be incredible. But leading a successful attack on the comm station would be a great way to impress both of them.

If you go into battle with Commander Cody, turn to page 23.

If you lead the attack on the comm station, turn to page 135.

"Let's move to the right," Falco says.

You cautiously make your way around the perimeter. Then you hear the unmistakable mechanical voice of a droid behind you.

"Stop, invaders!"

You whip around to see a small squad of droids charging at you. Falco opens fire, and the rest of you do the same. A droid in front of you goes down, but you're not sure if you hit it or if someone else in your squad did.

By the time you notice the droids attacking from behind it's too late. They make a tight circle around you.

"Drop your blasters, or we'll shoot."

Falco responds by decimating the droid with a shot from his blaster rifle. The droids return fire, and you scream out as he goes down. Splice runs to his side.

You were trained to go down fighting, but you know when you've lost. You and 44 drop your blasters. A droid marches up behind you and sticks a weapon in your back.

"March, prisoner," the droid commands.

You and 44 obey as the droids march you into their camp.

There's got to be a way to escape, you think desperately. This isn't over yet.

But as the droids march you past the machine you were sent to destroy, you overhear a command.

"The weapon is ready! Destroy the legion!"

You feel terrible. General Bandis trusted your squad with the mission to save the legion—and you failed.

THE END

"Let's try reprogramming the droids," you say.

The guard station is a makeshift hut located away from the fence. The two battle droids guarding it aren't even holding their blasters. They're sitting on the ground, and they seem to be drawing in the dirt.

You sneak up on them with Bruiser and Falco. As you get closer, you realize they're playing a game of banthas and mynocks, a simple game you used to play when you were a young clone. It was pretty much the only entertainment you had.

The droids don't seem to be having fun.

"I win! I got three banthas in a row!" one droid says.

"You lose! I'm banthas," says the other.

"No, you're mynocks!" the other droid yells.

You realize this is going to be easier than you thought. You whisper to Bruiser and Falco. "Stun them."

It just takes two quick plasma zaps before each droid goes limp. You drag them into the guard shelter and remove your gloves. You've never reprogrammed a droid before, but you learned all about droid wiring in training. You should be able to do it, and quickly get to work.

"Are you done yet?' Bruiser asks. "I could have blown up the whole place by now."

"Ready," you say. You switch both droids back on.

"I command you to commandeer that tank for us," you tell the droids.

"Tank? What tank? I thought I was banthas," one says.

The other droid runs out of the hut and starts running around in circles.

You sigh and leave the guard hut. You're about to tell Falco you'll storm the tank when you hear a strange sound from the battlefield. It's the same sound you heard when the hyperspace warp was activated.

Without the view from the cliff, it's tough to tell what's going on. But you can guess. There are no more clone troopers on the battlefield.

General Kenobi must have found a way to isolate the legion from the droid army. He's obviously taken them back to Ando Prime.

"What about us?" Bruiser asks.

"General Kenobi knows we're here," you say. "He'll come back for us."

You hope you're right. If not, you'll be stuck on an unknown planet with thousands of droids!

THE END

The EMF generator is located on the ground a few meters behind the machine. You run to it and take a look.

It's a black box about five meters long and two meters wide. Buttons on the top flash green to show that the device is working. You know from your training that there's no off switch—it's designed for protection. The only way to turn it off is to destroy it, as far as you can remember.

You take a detonator from your bag and hurl it at the generator, diving into the snow. There's a huge *BANG!* as the detonator explodes.

You sit up, feeling good about what you've done. But Vargus storms over to you.

"Rookie, what in the galaxy was that? I told you to deactivate it, not blow it up!"

You're not sure why he's upset—until you realize that the machine behind the force field is in pieces. You not only destroyed the EMF generator—you've destroyed the machine it was protecting.

"Sorry, Commander," you say.

Vargus shakes his head. "You're off demo for the rest of the mission," he tells you. "When this is all over, I'm sending you back to Kamino. You need to be reconditioned for a new specialization."

You've never felt lower than you do right now. Not only have you failed in front of your squad—but you don't get to blow stuff up anymore!

THE END

The results of your test flash on your screen.
DEMOLITIONS.

"I get to blow stuff up!" you say out loud. Then you quickly stop yourself. It's not like you to just shout things out like that. Clones just don't do that.

Then you realize the other trainees are talking, too. Everyone is excited to find out what his specialty is.

You're pretty happy with yours. Learning about weapons has always been one of your favorite things to study. And you know the clone army has some of the most advanced weaponry in the galaxy. To start with, every trooper gets assigned two plasma guns: a DC-15 blaster and a long range blaster rifle. Specialists like demolitions troopers have a wider array of weapons at their disposal. You've always wanted to get your hands on a thermal detonator, an unstable but highly effective grenade. Just one is powerful enough to blow up a starship's hull.

"Quiet down, please," Yan So says. "I will be assigning each of you to a squad. You will report for duty immediately. But first, I will announce the six trainees who have been assigned to accompany Commander Vargus on his special mission."

You hardly expect to be selected for the special

mission. So you're surprised when Yan So calls out your serial number.

"Commander Vargus is waiting for the six of you in the transport bay," Yan So tells you.

You exit the training room and head to the transport bay with the other squad members. You only recognize one of the six: a trooper you know as 57.

"So where do you think we're headed?" you ask him.

57 shrugs. "If it's a special mission, it's probably somewhere dangerous," he replies nervously. "I'm surprised they're trusting so many rookies to go."

"We're rookies, but we're still troopers," you say. "Besides, if we get into any danger, I'll just blow it up. I'm on demolitions."

"I'm supposed to be a medic," 57 says. "I wonder if I'll be the only one in the squad. I've patched up guys in simulation before, but I can't imagine doing it for real." He sounds more nervous than before.

"They wouldn't have made you a medic if you couldn't cut it," you tell him.

"I guess," 57 says. "Just try not to blow anything up if you can help it, okay?"

You arrive at the transport bay. A clone wearing a white armored suit with orange command symbols on it is standing in front of a gunship. There's a gray command sash strapped to his chest. His head is bald, and he's got a scar across his nose.

Commander Vargus shakes his head when he sees you. "Orange jumpsuits? I haven't worn one of those in ages," he says. "Get to troopers' quarters and get suited up—no helmets until we get to our destination. Meet me on the bridge in ten for a briefing."

Inside the ship you find your armor and gear inside a locker with your serial number on it. The body armor is made up of connected plates that fit your body like a glove. It's bright white. Most armies in the galaxy use camouflage in their armor so they can blend in with their environment. Clones don't need to do that. Clones don't hide. Your stark white uniforms strike fear into the hearts of your opponents.

You're pleased to find a special backpack in your locker filled with thermal detonators. The small orbs are made of silver metal. You can't wait until you get to toss one out for the first time.

It's time to head to the bridge. Commander Vargus introduces you to the rest of your squad. One is a seasoned medic named Splice, and 57 looks relieved to see him. Splice is quiet, and he has the same brown hair and standard haircut as the trainees. That's unusual for a trooper, you think. Most troopers change their hair in some way when they leave Kamino. It's the only way they have to stand out from the crowd.

The other trooper Vargus introduces is a little more lively. His name is Falco. He's cut his hair real short and his distinct helmet marks him as an Advanced Reconnaissance Fighter. ARFs are specially trained to work on special missions. They usually report directly to Jedi generals.

This must be a serious mission if we've got an ARF with us, you realize.

You're right.

"You're probably wondering why you've been assigned to Excelsior Company," Commander Vargus begins. "So I'll tell you. Twenty-four hours ago, Jedi General Po Bandis and five thousand troopers in the 313th Legion disappeared. We're going to find them."

"What do you mean, disappeared?" 57 asks. He looks pale.

"I mean, one minute they were on Ando Prime, the next minute they weren't," Vargus says.

He explains what happened.

The Separatists set up a base on the frozen planet of Ando Prime. General Bandis and the legion were sent to attack the post—a routine operation. Then they vanished. There were no emergency transmissions.

"How do you know they weren't just all . . . killed?" 57 asks.

"We don't know for sure," Vargus replies. "Members

of the Jedi Council sense that they are still alive—but not on Ando Prime."

"Could be a death trap," Falco mutters.

"Commander," you say. "A legion is comprised of five thousand men. Why is the Republic sending a small squad to find them?"

"Republic forces are stretched thin across the galaxy right now," Vargus answers. "The Council can't afford to lose another legion."

"But they can afford to lose us," 57 says. "Might as well call us the Expendables."

"Failure is not an option, trooper," Commander Vargus says firmly. "Here's the plan. We're landing at the coordinates of the last recorded transmission from General Bandis. Falco will recon the area and come back with a report. Then we'll decide on a course of action."

You spend the journey examining the weapons you've been assigned. You want to make sure they're working properly. Your plasma guns are powered by Tibanna gas, and you attach the magazines to your utility belt.

The gunship lands on Ando Prime, and Vargus sends out Falco. You go to the bridge and look out the window at the planet—the only place you've ever been besides Kamino. It's covered with snow that's being kicked up by a strong wind. You've been taught that your armor will keep you warm out there. You hope that's true.

You wait for what seems like a long time, and then Falco returns.

"I have discovered a service tunnel three kilometers from here," he reports. "I believe it may lead to the Separatist compound."

"Let's head out then," Vargus says.

You put on your helmet and Falco leads you and the squad to the service tunnel. You feel a slight chill, but your armor does a good job keeping you warm after all. But it's awkward stomping through the snow in your thick suit. The Kaminoans have designed it for battle, not for agility.

The service tunnel has been carved into the base of a small mountain. You remove a plasma-charged beam from your utility belt to light the way. Falco goes ahead to make sure the path is clear of traps or hidden enemies.

He contacts Commander Vargus via comlink.

"We've got a blockage up here," Falco reports. "Looks like the wall's partially caved in."

Vargus turns to you.

"Okay, Demo," he says. "Do your stuff."

You nod and race ahead, your heart pounding. You can't believe you're being called into action so quickly. You see Falco standing in front of two large boulders that are blocking the path.

"Should be easy work to take these out," Falco tells you. "Good luck."

He heads back to join the squad, leaving you alone. You open up your bag of explosives.

You studied tunnel explosives in training, but you're so excited, you can't keep your thoughts straight. A small pile of detonators would easily take down the boulders in one blast. Or, you could try a series of small strategically placed explosions.

If you go with one big blast, turn to page 40.
If you use a series of small strategically placed charges, turn to page 108.

"We'd better follow them," you say.

57 looks worried. "But Commander Vargus said—"

"I don't want to lose them now!" you say. "Come on. I'll contact Vargus after we find out where they're headed."

You dart out from behind the boulder, keeping an eye on the party of droids ahead of you. You do a quick count and see that there are twelve battle droids with Grievous. Each one looks the same—rust colored metal limbs, a barrel-shaped torso, and a long, thin face. Each droid carries a black blaster. Their weapons are not as long as your DC-15, but you know they can be just as deadly.

Grievous leads the squad into a gorge—the same gorge you've been ordered to investigate. It's narrow, and two tall mountain walls rise up on either side. There are no more boulders to give you cover now, but there are enough twists and turns in the path up ahead that you think you can pursue them without being spotted. You and 57 venture into the gorge and take cover behind a jagged ridge in the mountain wall.

"There is no sign of the army, General," one of the droids is saying.

"I can see that myself!" Grievous says angrily. Then

he coughs, making a horrible, hacking sound.

At that moment a shower of snow tumbles down the mountain and lands on top of a droid's head. The droid turns to the droid behind him.

"Hey, quit it!" he says.

"I didn't do anything!" the droid protests.

"Did, too," says the first droid. He scoops up some snow and throws it in the other droid's face.

Beside you, 57 laughs. You quickly cover his mouth, but it's too late. General Grievous spins around. Even though you're behind the rock, his dull, yellow eyes seem to be staring right at you.

"We're being followed!" he yells. "Blast them!"

Bam! Bam! Bam! Before you can react, the droid squad starts pummeling the ridge with lasers. Your cover starts to crumble in front of you. You somersault into the gorge and open fire.

Zap! Your aim is good, and you send one battle droid flying back into the snow. You see another droid fall and realize 57 is by your side.

Then . . . bam! A droid blast hits 57 in the arm, sending him tumbling. Angry, you take aim at the droid that hit 57 and point your DC-15 right at his torso, taking him down. You run and grab 57. There are too many droids for you to fight on your own. You have to retreat.

"What have we here? Republic clone troopers?"

Grievous is towering above you. He raises one of his four arms and knocks your DC-15 from your hands. You realize there is no way you can get away now.

"Capture them!" Grievous orders his squad.

"Told you we should have contacted Vargus," 57 says weakly.

You hate to admit it, but 57 is right.

THE END

"Our men have General Terrus and the droid army trapped in a quarry," General Bandis explains. "There are still some skirmishes happening on a hill next to the quarry. We need to drive all the remaining droid units into the quarry and contain them."

"Lead the way," Falco says.

You follow General Bandis and his squad away from the command center. You climb up a hill. When you reach the top and look down, you see an incredible battle scene.

Three Republic AT-TE walkers have blocked off the only entrance to the quarry. The armored attack vehicles look like giant metal bugs on six legs. Equipped with decimating laser cannons, they're tough and hard to take down.

Inside the quarry is a sea of rust colored metal droids firing away at the huge walkers. Several lines of clone troopers back up the AT-TEs, keeping the droids at bay.

General Bandis points to the next hill. "That's where we're needed."

You see that he's right. There's a strong concentration of droids battling clone troopers in close combat. There's no cover anywhere—it's an out-in-the-open brawl. The clones have the advantage, and they're forcing the droid units to the edge of the hill.

You and the squad race to the top of the hill to join the fray. General Bandis activates his lightsaber, and you hear a hum as the blade of green light extends from the handle. He quickly goes to work, slicing droids in half like he's cutting through butter.

A wave of heat explodes next to your head as a laser blast narrowly misses you. You turn to see a battle droid running toward you, firing his blaster wildly. You quickly raise your DC-15.

Wham! You hit the droid with a plasma bolt, and his head spins wildly around. Then he tumbles backward.

A surge of excitement flows through you. You just downed your first droid! You've dreamed of this day ever since you were a young clone.

But you don't have time to celebrate. A large droid made of bulky, gray metal armor stomps toward you. It's a super battle droid! They're a lot tougher than regular battle droids, and each one is equipped with double-laser cannons. This one is aiming his at you right now.

You don't have time to fire, and quickly somersault away to avoid the assault. You quickly recover and blast away with your DC-15, aiming for the droid's head.

The droid lifts its arm again to attack. Then it stops—and topples facedown into the dirt.

You're proud for a moment—you did it! Until you see the two clone troopers behind the super battle droid.

"Thanks," you say. Then you turn back to the battle.

General Bandis is charging a small group of battle droids, lightsaber held straight in front of him. You run to his side to help. Just as you reach him, the general collapses.

You're confused. You didn't see any fire hit the general. You jolt into medic mode and kneel over the general. His eyes are closed and his breathing is shallow.

A strange creature with a brown shell skitters out from under the general's tunic. Your mind races. Does the creature have something to do with what's wrong with General Bandis?

You move to chase after it, then stop yourself. General Bandis needs immediate help.

If you chase after the small creature, turn to page 92.

If you apply a bacta patch to General Bandis, turn to page 117.

Going after Falco could be dangerous—and Falco, your superior, told you to wait. You decide to let Commander Vargus know what's happening. You contact him using the comlink built into your helmet.

"Commander Vargus, Falco has been gone for more than an hour," you say. "Please advise course of action."

"Send me your coordinates, Sergeant," Vargus replies. "I'll bring the rest of the squad to meet you."

You give the coordinates, and then turn to 57 and 44.

"Squad's on the way," you say.

"That's good," 44 says.

There's nothing to do but wait. You hope Falco will turn up before Vargus does, but another half hour passes and there's no sign of him.

Finally, you see Vargus and the rest of the company in the distance.

"Over here!" 44 yells.

His voice echoes through the pass.

"Calm down, Slug," 57 says. "You'll cause an avalanche."

Then you hear another sound, and it's even louder than 44's yell. It's a sickening roar. You've never heard anything like it within the quiet walls of Tipoca City.

Vargus and the squad are charging at you, and you realize there must be something behind you. You spin around to see a huge mass of fur and claws jumping off the mountainside.

You and 57 dive out of the way, but 44 isn't fast enough. The creature lands on him. Then he jumps up and lifts 44 over his head.

It's a snow beast, you realize. They're a lot like the wampa beasts from the planet Hoth. The beast is big—at least twice as tall as you. Its long, black claws are as long as your face. Two dull, black eyes are set deep inside its furry face. Its mouth is a wide-open maw of sharp, jagged teeth.

Vargus is the first to arrive. He's shooting his powerful laser rifle at the beast.

"Drop him, you furball!"

Amazingly, the powerful plasma blasts don't seem to penetrate the beast's hide. He slings 44 over his shoulder and then stomps toward Vargus, roaring angrily.

You open fire with your DC-15, but the blaster doesn't do any damage. You watch helplessly as the creature swipes at Vargus with one of its massive paws.

The blow sends the commander falling back. Before he can get up, the beast stomps on Vargus.

Angry now, you race up to the beast, firing again and

again. You get the snow beast's attention. It drops 44 and heads back up the mountain where it came from.

57 races to Commander Vargus. His eyes are closed. You and the squad watch anxiously as 57 examines him.

"He's got some broken bones," 57 says. "We need a transport vehicle to get him back to the ship."

"I'll stay with the commander," Bruiser says.

Vargus opens his eyes. "Go with them, Bruiser," he says. "There might be more beasts out there."

"That's exactly why I should stay with you," Bruiser says.

"That's an order," Vargus says weakly.

It's up to you to organize the trek. You tell two troopers—44 and 16—to stay with 57 and Vargus. The other two—23 and 15—will come with you and Bruiser.

Soon the gunship is in sight. You pick up the pace.

ROOOAAAAAAR!

Three snow beasts emerge from the tundra, charging toward you. You can't get to the ship without encountering them.

"What's your command, Sergeant?" Bruiser asks.

You've got to do something. Turning and running isn't an option. You've got to attack them somehow. You've got four blasters, and there are three beasts. Will that be enough?

Then you remember you've got Bruiser with you.

There might be something in his bag of tricks powerful enough to take down three snow beasts.

If you order Bruiser to set off a sonic charge, turn to page 95.

If you order your troopers to attack with blasters, turn to page 119.

The sun on Ando Prime is setting as you head out to the coordinates Vylagos has given you. You can feel the temperature around you get colder, and hope you'll find some warmth when you get to the trading post.

You light the way with a high-intensity beam from your utility belt. 57 walks beside you.

"I remember reading about this planet," he says. "There are snow beasts here. Big ones. With lots of teeth."

"They're probably all sleeping," you say, trying to reassure him.

You hope you're right. Anything could be out here in the dark.

"If these coordinates are right, the trading post should be five kilometers west of here," Falco says. "If we're lucky, we'll be able to camp there for the night."

You plod on. The night gets colder and colder every minute. You're not sure how much longer your armor will be able to keep you warm in these conditions.

Finally, Falco announces that you have arrived.

"That's funny," he says. "These coordinates lead to that cave over there, in the mountainside."

"Maybe the trading post is inside," you say.

"Makes sense, right? Why would it be outside in the cold?"

"I'll check it out first," Falco says.

He enters the cave. Moments later, he comes running out backward, firing his blaster rifle.

A terrifying creature storms out of the cave after him. The beast is three times as tall as Falco and covered in white fur. It's got sharp claws and a mouth full of long fangs.

Falco's blasts are bouncing harmlessly off of the beast.

"Eighteen!" the ARF shouts.

"Got it!" you yell.

You activate a pulse grenade and lob it at the beast. Then you turn and run.

BOOM! You hear the explosion, but you don't look back. Falco races up beside you. You notice 57 is already half a kilometer ahead. He must have started running as soon as he saw the snow beast.

The adrenaline pumping in your body—and your anger toward Vylagos—keeps you warm on the long journey back to the Separatist outpost. You find Vargus and the others in the post's comm station. They're keeping watch over Vylagos.

Falco lunges for the scientist. "Lying traitor!" he yells. "He sent us into a trap!"

Vargus stops him. "He's no good to us dead," he says flatly. "It couldn't have been a great trap. You all made it back."

"Thanks to Eighteen," Falco says, and you're filled with pride again. It's almost worth everything you've been through.

"You guys get some rest," Vargus says. "In the morning, our scientist friend here is going to send you through that hyperspace warp to get that legion back."

You fall into a deep sleep, and in the morning you're ready to go. Vylagos doesn't seem happy about helping you—but the seven blasters trained on him must have convinced him. He hands Falco a small black box.

"You'll need to activate this when you're ready to come back," the Skakoan explains. "I've calibrated it so that every creature within one kilometer of the device will be transported back here."

Falco clips it to his belt. "Got it."

Vargus has chosen you, Falco, Splice, and a trooper named 44 to go through the hyperspace warp. 57 looks relieved to be off the hook.

You have to admit you're a little nervous. You know Vylagos can't be trusted. And you're not exactly sure where you're going, or if the whole hyperspace warp thing will work.

But you're a clone, and you go wherever you're

ordered. You've made it this far, you tell yourself. You'll make it back.

Vylagos activates the hyperspace warp, and you feel an incredible force pulling at your body. It's like every cell inside you is being turned inside out. It's a horrible feeling—and then it stops as quickly as it started.

You're not on Ando Prime anymore. You're on a rocky, barren planet, and you're in the middle of hundreds of clone troopers. One figure stands out—a man in a brown tunic and tall black boots. His skin is dark brown, and he's got four small horns growing from his forehead.

Falco races up to him. "General Bandis! We're from Excelsior Company. We've come to bring your legion back to Ando Prime."

"I'm afraid it might be too late for that," General Bandis says. "The droid army is about to destroy us."

Turn to page 146.

"We've got to get to Falco in one piece," you say. "No Podracing. We can walk the perimeter."

You know you've disappointed the troopers, but you have to let that just roll off of your back. Commanders don't get where they are because they're popular. They're leaders because they make the tough decisions that nobody else wants to make.

Still, it's a really long walk, and nobody's talking. You feel like you're never going to get to the other side.

A few hours later, you've made it. You look down the hilly slope of the canyon and see a military outpost. The snowy plain is dotted with long, one-story buildings made of metal. As Falco reported, it looks deserted.

"Falco, we're approaching the outpost," you call out over your comlink.

"Roger," Falco says. "I'm in building four-six-beta."

"We'll be there," you promise.

You head down the slope and search for the building Falco named. You enter to find Falco sitting at a table with two men.

One is a clone wearing the armor of a commander. His helmet is on the table in front of him.

The other is a man with a brown beard and mustache. He wears a brown tunic with a sash around the waist. You notice the handle of a weapon attached to the sash—a lightsaber handle.

He's a Jedi, you realize.

"'Bout time you all got here," Falco says.

The Jedi stands. "Hello, Sergeant," he says. "I am General Obi-Wan Kenobi. This is Commander Cody."

You can't believe your luck. Commander Cody? You've read about every one of his battles. There are thousands of clones in the galaxy. You never thought you'd get to meet Cody in person.

"It's an honor to meet you both," you say, taking off your helmet.

"We understand you are looking for the lost legion," Obi-Wan Kenobi said. "We could use your help. Commander Cody and I know where to find them."

Turn to page 47.

It doesn't take long for you to find out your assignment. Within minutes, the word MEDIC flashes on the screen in front of you.

You're surprised at first, but then you realize it makes sense. You've always liked learning about biology. You're fascinated with all the different kinds of creatures in the galaxy. And being a medic means you can help troopers who are hurt, which sounds pretty good to you.

You'll also be in the thick of battle, where every clone wants to be. You can study science and blast droids at the same time. It's the best of both worlds.

There is a murmur in the training room as the clones discover their assignments. The sound quickly stops when a clone commander marches into the room.

His white body armor with orange markings has a badge affixed to his chest plate to indicate his rank. He also wears a command sash across his chest. His head is completely bald, and he has a scar across the bridge of his nose.

"Commander Vargus is here to announce the troopers who will accompany him on the special mission Taun We spoke about," Yan So says.

"Right," says Vargus. "I need the following

troopers to follow me to the transport bay immediately."

He reads out six serial numbers—and yours is one of them! You can't believe it. The first mission you've been assigned to is a special mission for the Republic.

You stand up and follow Vargus and the other clones to the transport bay. He marches you up to a gunship with a deep hull and two wings on either side. Laser cannons are mounted on top of the wings.

"Get inside and get suited up," Vargus says. "Then meet me on the bridge in ten."

Inside the ship you find your serial number engraved on a locker. You open it up to see your body armor. You notice that your shoulder patches have orange circles on them and there is a thin orange stripe on your helmet— the mark of a medic.

You strap on your armor, leaving your helmet off. Then you attach a utility belt around your waist. It has ammo for your blaster, like a typical belt, but you've also got surgical tools attached: two vibroscalpels, one laser scalpel, and two laser cauterizers.

You've also got a medical kit that straps onto your back. You look through it and see a variety of bandages and bacta products to fight infection. There's also a portable FX-3 medical droid. The compact droid is shaped like a cylinder, with two arms that can be used to assist you during surgery. You're anxious to try it out, but you know you're due on the bridge.

You and the other rookies march down the narrow corridors of the gunship and report to the bridge. Commander Vargus is standing there, flanked by two clones.

One is wearing battered body armor. His hair is dyed bright blue, and he's got an arrow shaved into each side of his head.

The other clone has orange stripes down his arms, legs, and down the front of his chest. His hair is deep black and cut close to his head. You realize from his unique helmet that he's an Advanced Reconnaissance Fighter—an ARF. You know that ARFs have been specially trained on Kamino to go on special scouting missions. Only the very best clones get to be ARFs.

"Welcome to Excelsior Company," Vargus says. He nods to the blue-haired clone. "This is Dom, our demolitions man," he says.

"Call me Bruiser," Dom says. "I'm the guy who blows stuff up."

"And this is Falco," Vargus says, motioning to the ARF. "He'll be handling reconnaissance for this mission."

Falco just nods. Like most clones, he doesn't talk unless he's got something to say.

But Dom, you can tell, is different. "So boss, what

do you want to do with these rookies?" Dom asks. "My armor could use some polishing."

"We don't have time to haze rookies right now, Dom," Vargus says. "We've got a mission to complete."

Vargus moves to a console behind him, and a large screen on the bridge comes to life. A picture of a snow-covered planet pops up.

"This is Ando Prime," Vargus says. "The Republic received intelligence of a Confederacy outpost there. General Po Bandis and a legion of five thousand troopers traveled there to attack the enemy base—a routine operation. But twenty-four hours ago, the legion and their commander went missing. There were no emergency transmissions."

"How do five thousand troopers just go missing?" you ask.

"Nobody knows," Vargus replies. "That's where we come in. We're being sent to Ando Prime to investigate."

"So, we're being sent to a frozen planet where five thousand men have vanished without a trace?" Dom asks. He laughs. "Might as well call us the Expendables."

Expendable. That doesn't sound good. But it might explain why six rookies were chosen for such an important mission.

If we vanish, they'll just send another squad to replace us, you realize. And another . . . and another. That's what being a clone is all about. If anything happens to you, the Kaminoans will just step up production in the lab.

You shake the thought from your head. You're a medic now. It's up to you to make sure your squad completes the mission in one piece.

"We'll be landing at the coordinates of the last recorded transmission from General Bandis," Vargus says. "Falco, I want you and the medic to do the first sweep of the area. There could be injured troopers out there who need help."

You nod. You're going to be the first rookie in your squad to set foot on Ando Prime, and it's a good feeling. You're going to set foot on another planet for the first time in your life!

The gunship's hyperdrive gets you to Ando Prime pretty quickly. When the ship lands, you see the planet really is covered with snow and ice as far as you can see. You put on your helmet, and you and Falco step out into the bitter cold.

You've landed in some kind of Republic command center. There is a makeshift comm hut surrounded by several tents. But it appears to be deserted.

Falco's instructions are brief. "Follow me, stay behind me, and do what I tell you."

You don't argue. You follow Falco as he checks the hut and every tent to see if anyone is inside. Then he walks the perimeter of the area. Finally, he stops.

"There's a trail here," he says. "I want to check it out."

You keep following, your feet crunching on the snowy trail. Small hills rise up around you, and there is a mountain in the distance.

Suddenly, Falco puts an arm out to stop you.

"There's something up ahead," he says quietly.

You look past him to see what looks like a pile of white fur on the trail in front of you. Falco slowly moves closer, and you realize it is a person wrapped in fur robes. You wonder if it is a Talid, the native species on Ando Prime.

Falco approaches the Talid, his DC-15 blaster drawn.

"Who are you?" Falco asks.

"Please," the Talid says weakly. "My Podracer crashed fifty meters from here. I tried to walk back to my village, but my leg is hurt."

Falco turns to you. "Seems harmless," he says. "Let's keep going."

"But I can help him," you say.

"We've got to stick to the mission," Falco tells you.

If you agree with Falco and move on, turn to page 21.
If you help the injured Talid, turn to page 13.

"Let's move!" you yell as you and 57 race off after the fleeing figure.

He runs to the last building and darts behind it. As you turn the corner, you see he is heading for a droid fighter plane. He turns and fires a droid blaster at you. A sharp pain hits your leg. At close range, the droid blast feels like you've been smacked with a wall of concrete.

The attack makes you angry. You dive forward, grabbing onto the folds of his brown robe. He stumbles, and you both go down.

He struggles, trying to get up, but 57 grabs his arms. The droid blaster falls out of his hands.

"Please, stop!" he wails. He speaks in a strange accent, and his voice sounds muffled inside the metal armor. "I will not harm you!"

"Too late for that," you say.

You let go, and 57 pulls him to his feet.

"Who are you?" you ask.

"My name is Vylagos," he replies. "I am a Skakoan engineer."

Commander Vargus and the rest of the squad arrive.

"Good work," Vargus says. He turns to the

rookies. "Fan out and make sure the rest of the buildings are clear."

"Eighteen is hurt," 57 says, and you suddenly remember the pain in your leg.

"It's nothing," you say. "He got off a shot before we took him down."

Vargus nods to the building behind you. "Splice can take care of you inside. Dom, help Five-Seven secure the prisoner."

Soon you're up on a table, and Splice has removed the armor from your leg. Your shin looks like a purple balloon.

"I can clean it and bandage it, but it'll take a while to heal," Splice tells you. In a way, you're proud of your injury. You feel like a real trooper now.

On the other side of the room, Vargus is questioning Vylagos. The Skakoan is seated in a chair, guarded closely by Dom. Dom reaches to take off the engineer's helmet.

"Please, no!" the Skakoan protests. "If you remove the helmet, I will not survive."

Dom scowls, but Vargus motions for him to back off.

"Tell me what you're doing here," Vargus demands.

"I was hired by the Confederacy," Vylagos begins.

"Separatist slime!" Dom interrupts.

"I do not get involved in politics," Vylagos says

simply. "I am an engineer. I will work for whomever hires me. Right now, it appears that I am no longer employed. I will freely tell you what you need to know."

"Let's hear it, then," Vargus says, a little impatiently.

"The Confederacy hired me to build a hyperspace warping device, one capable of instantly warping large numbers of droid units anywhere in the galaxy," the scientist replies. "I believe they were planning an attack on Coruscant."

It's a brilliant plan, you realize. Coruscant is the seat of the Republic government. It's heavily guarded. A surprise attack like Vylagos describes would probably help the Separatists win the war.

"Does it work?" Vargus asks.

"Apparently so," Vylagos answers. "Your Republic general found the base and launched an attack. The device was accidentally activated. Fortunately I fled the base before the attack. When I returned, both the Republic legion and the droid army were gone."

"Gone?" Vargus asked.

"Transported through a hyperspace wormhole created by the machine," Vylagos explains.

Vargus frowns. "So they're all on Coruscant? Wouldn't we have heard something?"

"The machine was activated accidentally," Vylagos explained. "The armies appear to have been transported somewhere beyond the Outer Rim."

"So how do we get them back?" Vargus asks.

"The legion can return from the other side, but they must be present in the same location they arrived at when they were transported. You would be wise to send a party to the other side to lead them back through," Vylagos says. "I can restart the machine—for a price, of course."

"I've got an idea," Dom interjects. "How about you restart the machine, and we let you keep your helmet on."

The threat silences the Skakoan. Vargus turns to you.

"How's your leg, Recon?" he asks. "Feel like going through that wormhole?"

You don't answer right away. Vylagos could be lying. Whoever goes through that wormhole could be headed into a trap. Your injury is the perfect excuse to stay behind.

Then again, if you really can rescue the legion, you'll be a hero when the dust settles.

If you stay behind, turn to page 138.

If you go through the wormhole, turn to page 158.

Since you're not sure what will happen if you target the reactor, you decide to place charges in the four corners.

"We need to get here, here, here, and here," you say, pointing to the blueprint.

"No problem," Falco says. "Follow me."

You step out of the storage room and climb up a metal staircase. You end up on a metal catwalk that goes around the perimeter of the factory. Down below, you can see droids being assembled on a moving conveyor belt. Falco was right. There are thousands of them.

"Stay quiet, and they won't notice us," Falco says. "They're not curious, and they usually keep their eyes on their work."

You think you must be pretty conspicuous in your white armor, but Falco seems to be right. You cautiously make your way to the first corner of the factory and put the detonator in place.

You reach the second corner just as successfully. When you get to the third corner, the detonator slips out of your hands.

You cringe as it bounces off of the metal catwalk and lands on the head of a droid worker below. You hold your breath, hoping the droid won't notice. But you aren't so lucky. The droid looks up.

"Clone troopers!" he cries.

"Time to go," Falco says. He talks into his comlink. "Commander Vargus, we have been detected. Repeat. We have been detected."

You follow Falco up another stairway. Battle droids are swarming around you now, trying to stop you. You emerge outside into the snow.

"You might want to detonate those charges now," Falco tells you.

"Right," you say.

You press the remote, and a loud explosion rocks the factory. But thousands of droids are already pouring out onto the planet's surface.

You race to Commander Vargus and the rest of the crew.

"Retreat!" Vargus yells when he sees the onslaught of droids.

You charge across the snow with your squad, hoping you can get back to your ship. But your clone armor slows you down.

You're angry with yourself. If only you had targeted the power source instead!

THE END

If that creature bit General Bandis, you'll need to use its venom to make an antidote. You spring up and chase after it, dodging laser blasts as you run.

The creature has about twenty small legs under its shell, and it's fast. You finally catch up and quickly grab it with one hand. A wicked-looking stinger extends out from under the shell. Luckily, your armor will protect you.

You race back to General Bandis, grabbing a trooper on the way.

"I need cover!" you tell him. "The general's down!"

"No problem," the trooper replies. He stands guard over you as you kneel down and get to work.

In your training, you learned how to synthesize antivenom. You just hope you have enough equipment in your pack to make it work. First order of business is to zap the creature with your blaster. Then you use a scalpel to extract venom from the creature's stinger.

You work as quickly as you can. It's not easy to do with laser fire whizzing past your head. But with the help of your portable FX-3 medical droid, you have a crudely synthesized antivenom. You take a deep breath before you inject it into General Bandis.

"Hope this works," you mutter.

To your surprise, it does. General Bandis opens his eyes.

"I feel like I've been gored by a tauntaun," he says, his voice hoarse.

You hold up the dead creature. "Actually, it was this."

General Bandis groans and gets to his feet. "Whatever you did, thank you," he says. He looks over the hilltop.

"Super battle droids are breaching the line at the quarry!" he cries. "Troops, move out!"

General Bandis leads the troops back to the entrance of the quarry. You are eager to blast more droids, but the super battle droids have downed some of the troops. You're a medic, and your job right now is to heal, not fight.

You quickly go to work, cleaning and closing wounds of the injured troopers. General Bandis and his men quickly take control of the quarry again, driving back the super battle droids.

With the droid army trapped again, General Bandis orders a demolitions squad to close off the quarry with a rockslide. Then he leads the troops back to the comm station, where you first encountered him. He turns to Falco.

"Can you get us out of here now?" he asks.

"Think so," Falco says.

You brace yourself as Falco activates the homing device Vylagos gave him. That strange, horrible feeling hits you again, but it stops just as quickly.

A blast of cold wind hits you in the face, and you realize you're back on Ando Prime. You've been transported back near the machine. The thousands of men in the legion now cover the planet's snowy hills.

Commander Vargus rushes up to General Bandis.

"General Bandis! You made it!" he says.

"Thanks to your brave squad," General Bandis says. "One of them saved my life."

You realize he's talking about you, and you stand up a little straighter.

General Bandis turns to you. "If it's all right with your commander, I'd like you to serve as a medic in my company."

"Excelsior Company will miss him, but I won't refuse you, General," Vargus says.

"Thank you, General," you say. "I won't let you down."

It's a real honor to serve under a Jedi general. Your future as a clone trooper looks bright.

THE END

You suddenly remember something you read—
wampas are sensitive to certain sound frequencies. If
these beasts are similar, they might be sensitive, too.

"Bruiser, set a sonic charge now," you say.

"Sonic?" Bruiser asks.

"Trust me," you say.

Bruiser quickly reaches for his pack. He pulls out a
small metal globe, presses a button, and hurls it at the
beasts.

You don't hear anything, but the sonic blast does
exactly what you'd hoped. The snow beasts roar and
get on all fours, racing away over the hills.

"I can't believe that worked, rookie," Bruiser
says. It doesn't sound like much of a compliment. But
coming from Bruiser, you know it is.

"Come on," you say. "We've got to get back to the
commander."

Inside the ship's bay is a BARC speeder that belongs
to Falco. It's a single-man vehicle, but you rig up a
panel on the back so you can bring Vargus back. You
send Bruiser out to retrieve Vargus. You stay behind
with 23 and 35 in case the beasts come back.

Bruiser leaves, and it isn't long before you hear the
vehicle speeding back to the ship. You open the bay.

The BARC driver takes off his helmet. It's 57.

"Bruiser sent me back with Vargus so I can patch him up," 57 tells you. "He's coming back on foot with the others."

"Good," you agree. "Let's get the commander to medical."

In the medical bay, 57 sets the commander's broken bones with the help of a portable FX-3 medical droid. While 57 is at work, Bruiser returns with 44 and 16.

"We would have been back sooner if it wasn't for Slug here," Bruiser reports, nodding at 44.

"Any sign of the beasts?" you ask.

Bruiser shakes his head. "Sonic charge must have spooked them all. How's the commander?"

"I was just about to check on him," you say.

You find Commander Vargus sitting up in the medical bay. His eyes are open and he looks alert.

"How are you feeling, Commander?" you ask.

"Fine," he replies. "But Patch says I've got to stay off my leg for a couple of days."

You realize Vargus is talking about 57. He's got a nickname now, too. You're starting to feel a little left out.

"Just got a transmission from Falco," Vargus says. "He's located the Separatist outpost. Says it's deserted, but thinks there are some things there worth investigating. At first light, I want you to lead a squad out there, Sergeant. Take Bruiser with you and two other troopers."

"Yes, sir," you say.

You leave the medical bay, and Vargus's words sink in. He's trusting you to lead a mission. That's better than a nickname. Well, almost better.

The next morning, you head out with 23 and 35. You feel bad leaving 44 with the commander, but you know he'll only slow you down. You've got the coordinates Falco left, and a holographic map of the planet so you can determine the best route there.

You decide to avoid the mountain pass in case the snow beasts return. There's a wide plain you can cross that leads to what looks like some kind of canyon or quarry. The outpost is on the other side.

You walk all morning. At least, you think it's morning. The sun might be shining up above somewhere, but it can't penetrate the gray clouds in the atmosphere. A light snow falls as you trek across the plain.

Finally, you reach the canyon. It's much wider and deeper than you realized. When you peer over the edge, you discover something else.

There's a ridge at the top of the canyon that goes all the way around—it's a racetrack! The ridge ends abruptly in a steep cliff that drops all the way to the canyon's bottom. Along the track you can see what look like two abandoned Podracers.

"A Podracing track!" Bruiser says. He sounds like an excited, young clone. "I always wanted to try Podracing!"

"We could use them to get across the canyon," 23 suggests.

"Podracers have a one-man cockpit," you say. "We'll have to walk around."

You know that walking around the canyon will take a long time—but it's the only way to get to the camp. There's no way you can scale up and down the canyon's steep sides.

"Come on," 35 says. "Podracers have powerful engines. We can fit two of us on each one."

If you order your men to walk around the canyon, turn to page 78.

If you agree to ride the Podracers across the canyon, turn to page 18.

You don't want to take any chances. With the help of your FX-3 medical droid you prep the Skakoan for surgery. Falco leaves to recon the rest of the compound.

Then you pick up your scalpel and stare at the abdomen. You take a deep breath.

You make your first incision and discover you're in the wrong place—you've revealed what appear to be lungs.

"Vital signs declining," the FX-3 reports.

You quickly work to stabilize the Skakoan. You're successful—almost. The Skakoan is alive, but he's slipped into a deep coma. You administer the bacta injection but it's too late for that now.

"Is there anything I can do to revive him?" you ask the droid.

"Negative," the droid responds.

You put your helmet back on and go outside to find Falco.

"He's in a coma," you tell the ARF. "I might be able to help him if we get to a medical bay on the ship. But I suspect he needs a Skakoan medic in the end. I don't know what's going on under that skin."

"Squad's on the way," Falco says. "I found something interesting."

He leads you behind one of the buildings to a strange machine. You're not sure what it does. Vargus and the squad arrive and Vargus sends a report to his superiors. They think it might have something to do with the legion's disappearance. They tell Vargus they're sending a Republic scientist to examine it, but he can't get there for a few weeks.

Excelsior Company is stuck on Ando Prime until the scientist gets there. You manage to keep the Skakoan stable on the ship, but you can't wake him from his coma. It's frustrating. You have a feeling that whatever that machine is, the Skakoan could tell you what it does.

THE END

The results of your test flash on your screen.

SPECIALTY: COMMAND
UNIT: EXCELSIOR COMPANY
REPORT IMMEDIATELY
TO COMMANDER VARGUS
ON THE TRANSPORT BAY.

You stare at the screen for a few seconds, blinking
in disbelief. Command? You? Not only that, but you've
been assigned to Commander Vargus. That means
you've been chosen for the special mission Taun We
spoke about.

You stand up and notice five other troopers do the
same. They must be the rest of the rookies chosen for
the mission. You give them a nod as you head to the
transport bay.

Your mind races as you walk through the silent
corridors. Command. You still can't believe it.
You'll start out as a sergeant, like all troopers in
the command chain do. Then, depending on your
performance, you'll rise in the ranks. First you'll be
promoted to lieutenant, then captain, and then finally,
commander. Just like Commander Cody.

Of course, you've got to impress your superiors,

you know. You've got to perform well, and survive countless battles. But someday, maybe, you'll get there. You'll be able to wear the special command symbols on your armor, and maybe even a command sash or shirt to indicate your rank.

But the best thing about being in command is that finally you'll get a name. You won't be a number anymore. Seasoned clones give each other nicknames, and clone commanders all get to choose names. It's too bad Cody is already taken, you think. You like the sound of that.

You're going over names in your head when you arrive at the transport bay. Commander Vargus is standing in front of a Republic gunship. He's got a shaved head and a scar across the bridge of his nose. He looks just like you imagine a commander should look.

"Which one of you is Sergeant Eighteen?" he asks.

You step forward. "I am, sir."

"Take your men to the troopers' quarters and get suited up," he instructs. "You'll find an outline of the mission on your comm screens."

"Yes, sir!" you say. You turn to the rest of the rookies. "Move out, men!"

You march into the gunship, followed by the troopers. In the quarters, you each have a locker with your serial number. You suit up into your white body armor and then take a seat on the bench. As instructed, you activate your comm screen and review the mission details.

> *Three days ago, the 313th Legion of the Republic arrived on Ando Prime to perform a routine attack on the Separatist outpost there. Twenty-four hours ago, the legion disappeared. There were no emergency transmissions, although we have verified all comm equipment is operational. The Jedi Council senses that the legion is alive, but in some kind of danger. Excelsior Company's mission: to travel to Ando Prime and determine the whereabouts of the 313th Legion.*

The rest of the troopers read along with you in silence. Then one speaks up. You know him as 44.

"Aren't there five thousand men in a legion?" he asks. "How could they all just vanish? It doesn't make sense."

"That's why they're sending us," you reply. "We'll find out what happened."

"But that's five thousand men," 44 repeats. "We're only a squad of six troopers. What happens if we disappear, too?"

"They'll just make more of us."

The voice is coming from the doorway. It belongs to a trooper in battered armor. His hair is dyed blue and has shapes shaved into the sides.

"They named us Excelsior Company, but they might as well call us the Expendables," the trooper says.

You stand up. "Sergeant Eighteen, sir," you say with a salute.

The trooper grins. "Sergeant, eh?" he says. "Name's Dom, but you can call me Bruiser. I'm the demolitions man in this company."

Dom turns and strolls down the corridor.

"See? We're expendable," 44 says.

The other troopers look worried. As sergeant, you should probably keep their spirits up.

"He's just riding us because we're rookies," you say. "Don't let him get to you."

Even in hyperdrive, it's a long trip to Ando Prime. You pass the time reading all the data you can about the planet. Then you decide to do something you've been waiting ten years to do.

You borrow a scalpel from trooper 57, the troop medic. You use it to carefully cut away your hair. You don't want to go completely bald—that would be too close to Vargus. But you manage to give yourself a decent crew cut. You examine yourself in the mirror, and decide you like it. You remember Bruiser's blue hair and wonder where he got the dye. You've always liked the color red.

Finally, you land on Ando Prime. Vargus introduces you to your other squad member, an Advanced Reconnaissance Fighter named Falco.

"This is the site of the last recorded transmission from General Bandis," Commander Vargus tells you. "General Bandis said he was nearing the location of the enemy outpost. We're going to begin our search here. Falco, I want you to take some men with you. Eighteen, Five-Seven, and Forty-Four."

"You want me to babysit?" Falco asks, and Dom chuckles.

"These men all need some field experience," Vargus replies. "Do a sweep of the area and report back."

You put on your helmet, make sure your blaster is loaded, and follow Falco outside the gunship. Ando Prime is a frozen planet. There is snow as far as you can see. Falco marches ahead without a word. Your body armor keeps you warm, but your new armor is stiff, and it's tough to keep up with Falco's pace.

44 is having the hardest time of it. He's twenty meters behind the rest of you, and he can't seem to catch up. Falco stops and calls back to him.

"Get moving, slug!" he yells. "If you get stranded out here, it's not my fault."

You know it's weird, but you actually feel jealous. 44 now has a nickname—Slug. Sure, it's a lousy nickname, but it's way better than a number.

You plod on through the deep snow. Now you know why the Kaminoans designed you to be a perfect specimen of physical conditioning. Not many humanoids could tolerate a frozen trek like this.

Finally, Falco stops at the base of a mountain.

"You three wait here," he tells you. "I need to proceed alone. If there's a droid base on the other side of this mountain pass, we'll be spotted if all four of us walk into it. I'll be right back."

Falco's logic makes sense. You watch him disappear into the mountain pass.

Then you wait.

Minutes pass. You watch the snow fall around you in silence. Conversation skills are not part of your training on Kamino.

An hour goes by, and you wonder if Falco is playing some kind of trick on you. You've heard about troopers hazing rookies. That's it, you convince yourself. He's probably back at the ship, laughing it up with Dom.

Then you hear Commander Vargus in your comlink.

"Sergeant, what's your status?" he asks.

"Falco has moved ahead," you say. "He's asked us to wait to avoid detection."

"That's Falco for you," Vargus says. "Always going it alone. Let me know when you hear from him."

"Roger, sir," you reply.

"What was all that?" 44 asks. "How come you didn't tell him Falco's been gone for an hour?"

"He didn't ask," you say.

"Falco said he would be right back," 44 says. "Something's gotta be wrong."

"I think Slug's right," says 57. "You should tell Vargus what's up."

You're a sergeant, you tell yourself. You're supposed to be telling your men what to do, not the other way around. If you call Vargus, he'll think you can't hack it. You think we should go find Falco. That's what a commander would do.

If you go after Falco, turn to page 28.
If you contact Vargus, turn to page 70.

Your training kicks in—and you're lucky it does. You remember that using explosives in a tunnel—especially a service tunnel—is always tricky business. A huge charge could cause the whole tunnel to collapse. You decide to play it safe.

You examine the boulders and determine the weakest point. Then you place one thermal detonator in that exact spot. If you're right, you should blast a path big enough for the squad to go through.

You activate the detonator—and run. You're about ten meters away when the charge goes off.

BOOM!

You stop and turn around. A cloud of dust swells up behind you. You race back to the blockage to see if you're successful.

The single charge worked perfectly. There's a trooper-sized hole in the center of the boulders. You quickly move pieces of broken rubble out of the way.

"All clear!" you call down the tunnel.

The squad appears, led by Vargus and Falco. The commander nods.

"Good work, rookie," he says.

You feel proud—even though he's called you a rookie. You're just happy that your first blast was successful.

The company slowly progresses down the tunnel as Falco scouts the path ahead of you. It's dark, and you're starting to feel warm—it's a lot different than the planet's frozen surface.

The tunnel is a long one, and after several hours Commander Vargus has you stop to eat your rations. You take off your helmet, and sweat trickles down your neck.

You're eating a protein block when Falco returns.

"You're not gonna believe what's at the end of this tunnel," he says. "It's a droid factory. A big one. They're making thousands of them in there."

Commander Vargus gets a gleam in his eyes.

"So where does the tunnel end up?" Vargus asks.

"It leads to some kind of storage room," Falco reports. "As far as I can tell, the service tunnel isn't used anymore. We could get inside without being detected. But there are a lot of droids in there. I don't think the ten of us can take them down."

"I don't want to take them down," Vargus replies. "I want to blow them up."

You like the sound of that.

"How do you want me to proceed?" you ask.

"I know you don't have a complete arsenal with you, so you'll have to determine the best location to set your charges," Vargus says. "You can set them remotely, right?"

You nod.

"Go with Falco to scout out the best spot for your charges," Vargus says. "I'll get the rest of the squad to the surface, away from the blast. Contact me on the comlink before you set anything off."

"The main concentration of droids seems to be in the assembly room," Falco says. "You should be able to get to the surface without being detected."

Falco nods to you. "Come on. You've got a factory to blow up."

You put your helmet back on and follow Falco through the tunnel, your blood pounding with excitement. You've never seen a battle droid in person before, and now you're going to see thousands of them.

The tunnel ends at a metal door. Falco puts his ear against it and then slides it aside. He looks around.

"All clear," he says.

You step out from behind him into a big concrete room. It's filled with metal shelves loaded with boxes of wires, springs, and what appear to be metal droid pieces.

"I'm going to try to find a computer panel to see if we can get a schematic of this place," Falco says. "Stick close."

You don't argue. Falco slowly makes his way across the storage room, using the shelves for cover. You can see a small computer hub next to the doorway.

Falco's about to move forward when the door slides open. Two battle droids step through, and you and Falco freeze.

The droids walk into the storage room. They walk stiffly on their metal limbs.

"More bolts. More bolts," one of the droids says.

"Nuts. I thought we need nuts," the other droid says.

"You're nuts," says the first droid. "It's bolts we need."

The droids are on the other side of the shelf. You hold your breath, hoping they don't see you.

"Nuts!"

"Bolts!"

While the droids argue, Falco slowly pushes a box of nuts and a box of bolts toward them. The droids notice.

"Let's bring both," says one.

"Good idea," says the other.

The two droids pick up the boxes and walk out. Falco turns to you.

"Not the brightest stars in the galaxy," he says, and you have to agree. You expected the battle droids to be fierce, but they seem pretty comical.

"Don't underestimate them, though," Falco says as though he's reading your mind. "They're not smart, but they pack plenty of ammo, and they don't get tired."

Falco quickly moves to the computer port. He takes a small device from his belt and plugs it in. He presses some buttons, and then a blueprint of the factory shows up on his screen.

"Take a look at this," he tells you.

You examine the blueprint. The factory is shaped like a simple rectangle. The main supports are in the four corners of the building. You could set charges in each corner, but you'll have to get all around the building without being seen.

That's one option. You search the blueprints for another.

Then you spot it. The factory is powered by a small lithium reactor located in the sub-basement. If you explode the reactor, you might just be able to create a charge big enough to take down the factory in one blast.

"What's it gonna be, rookie?" Falco says.

You don't answer right away. This is a much bigger job than blowing up some boulders. You want to make sure you get it right.

If you place charges in the four corners of the factory, turn to page 90.

If you place charges in the factory's power source, turn to page 154.

The figure might be a Talid, but it isn't shooting at you. Besides, what would a sniper be doing out in the open?

"Hold your fire!" you yell.

The figure hears you and turns. He definitely looks like a Talid. He waves his arms and shouts something in a language you don't understand.

You hear a thundering sound and see three huge beasts circling around the building next to you. The creatures are running on strong hind legs. Each one is covered with fur and has a long, curved tail. The beasts are saddled, and each one carries a Talid rider. These must be the tantas you read about.

Bam! Bam! Bam!

The Talid shoot as they ride toward you. Your blaster goes flying out of your hand.

They know they can't defend themselves against our blasters, you realize. Pretty smart.

You take a flying dive after your blaster, but one of the tantas lunges at you. You spin around but the giant beasts have you and your men trapped inside a circle.

You think quickly, sizing up your situation. You could try to take the Talid on in hand-to-hand combat, but their slugthrowers are pointed squarely at you. At close range, they might be able to do some real damage.

You've got to think about the safety of your men. You raise your hands in the air.

"We surrender," you say.

The tantas paw at the snow, and the Talid riders motion for you to move. You're not sure where they're taking you, or what they want.

With the comlink down, there's no way to contact Commander Vargus. Your only hope is that he'll send a search party after you.

You're starting to wish you had contacted Vargus when you had the chance.

THE END

You don't want to take the risk.

"Hold on," you tell 57.

You contact Vargus. "Commander, there is an unknown subject fleeing the site. Awaiting orders."

"Engage pursuit," Vargus tells you. "We'll be there soon to back you up."

"Over," you say. Then you and 57 chase after the fleeing figure. He races behind one of the buildings. You turn the corner and see him climbing into a droid fighter—a small starship with a round cockpit and long, sleek wings.

Instinctively, you fire your blaster and 57 does the same. But your plasma bolts don't do much damage to the starfighter. The engine roars to life, and the droid fighter speeds off into the sky.

"Slugnuts," you mutter. You've let him get away. If only you had listened to 57 and acted quickly.

Captain Vargus and the squad run up to you.

"We saw the starfighter," Vargus says. "Guess he got away."

"Yes, Commander," you reply.

Dom snorts. "That's what you get when you send a rookie to do a man's job."

Dom's words burn you up, but you know he's right.

You feel pretty down right now. Thankfully, Vargus doesn't give you a hard time.

"Let's search the base," he says. "There might be more of them hiding."

You and the squad search each of the buildings, but the place is deserted. The only unusual thing you find is a strange-looking machine. In all of your studies, you've never seen anything like it. Vargus doesn't recognize it, either.

"There's a Republic base on a planet not far from here," Vargus says. "Let's take it there. They might be able to figure out what it does. I have a feeling it has something to do with what happened to the legion."

You do, too. You also have a feeling that guy in the armor could have told you what it was—but it's too late for that now.

THE END

You decide you don't have time to go chasing the creature. You open up the general's tunic and see an angry red bite on his abdomen. You guess that's what is causing the problem—some kind of venomous bite. You immediately apply a bacta patch, hoping that will have a counter-effect on the venom.

You pick up General Bandis and carry him back down the hill, where he'll be safe. But the bacta patch doesn't work. General Bandis is unconscious, and soon he starts to burn up with a fever. You try everything you know to bring the fever down, but General Bandis just seems to be getting worse.

A loud explosion booms from the top of the hill. You look up to see a line of super battle droids storming into battle. A small tank rolls up behind them. They've broken out of the quarry!

The top of the tank pops open, and a humanoid with a scaly, reptilian face peers out of the tank. A swirled, bony horn grows directly from the top of his head. You realize he's a Koorivar—this must be General Terrus.

"Storm the hill!" he bellows. The super battle droids open fire, and your mouth goes dry as you see several clone troopers fall.

The tide of the battle is turning. In the chaos, you can't see Falco or the rest of your squad. Without General Bandis, you feel that the 313th Legion will be lost.

There's only one thing you can do—your job. You grab your medical kit and run up the hill to take care of the fallen troopers.

THE END

"Open fire!" you yell.

The air explodes with plasma blasts as all four of you fire on the beasts. This enrages them. They descend upon your group.

Bruiser removes his pack of explosives, but before he can remove the more serious weapons from inside it, one of the snow beasts swats it away. It lands in the middle of a group of three more beasts that are coming to join the fray.

You're not sure why they're attacking, but you realize that doesn't really matter. You're outnumbered, and your weapons aren't any help.

"Retreat!" you yell.

You turn and run, scanning the landscape. It's fairly barren, but there's a snowy bluff a few hundred meters west. You can head there and decide your next move.

Bruiser, 23, and 35 follow you to the bluff. You're glad they're all safe, at least. For some reason, the snow beasts haven't followed you.

But they haven't left, either. They're pacing back and forth in front of the ship.

"Rotten furballs," Bruiser mutters. You can tell he's still stung about losing his pack.

"It's like they're keeping us from the ship on purpose," you say.

"Maybe we landed in their territory," 23 pipes up, and you realize that makes sense.

"Do you think that's what happened to the lost legion?" 35 asks.

"Not likely," you say. "We're talking five thousand troopers. It would take a lot of snow beasts to take down that many troopers without a trace."

You take stock of your situation.

Vargus is injured, and needs help. You can't get back to your ship. It's going to be night in a few hours, and you're not sure if your armor will protect you from the extreme cold then.

You wish you knew what to do, but you don't have a clue. Maybe Bruiser was right.

You are the Expendables after all!

THE END

You don't want to get trapped in the cave.

"There's a path up the mountainside," you say. "Follow me to higher ground!"

Heading to higher ground is normally a good idea—if your enemy is below you. As you race up the mountain, you hear another shot.

"Hey!"

44 cries out as something slams into his leg and he falls backward. 57 rushes to his side. He picks up a small, round piece of metal in the snow.

"It's a slug," 57 reports.

Now you know you're not dealing with droids. They don't use such primitive weapons. It must be the Talid. You remember reading something about them being overprotective of the junk they like to collect.

"This path must lead to a Talid stockpile," you say. "They must have snipers guarding it."

You spin around and aim your blaster in the direction of the last shot that was fired. You know you have the advantage. The Talid's armor can't withstand shots from a plasma gun.

Then . . . *bam!* A slug hits your blaster, tearing it from your hands. You dive into the snow to grab it but you see that the gas cartridge has been damaged.

That sniper knows what he's doing, you realize. But you're not finished yet.

"Five-Seven, throw me your blaster!" you yell.

He obeys, tossing it to you.

Bam!

The sniper hits it clear out of the sky.

You've only got one weapon left—44's. He's still holding his leg, groaning. You move to take his blaster, but it's too late.

You're surrounded by Talid. Their stocky bodies are wrapped in thick furs. Their faces are completely covered with eye protection and layers of scarves. Some of them have braided white hair sticking out from under their hoods.

You slowly take off your utility belt and hold it in front of you.

"Trade?" you say. With luck, maybe that's all the Talid want.

You're not so lucky. They indicate for you to follow them. 57 helps 44 to his feet.

The reality hits you—you're a prisoner of the Talid now.

You wish you had contacted Commander Vargus when you had the chance.

THE END

You wait until Grievous and the droids are out of hearing distance. Then you contact Vargus using the comlink built into your helmet.

"Enemy squad spotted, Commander," you report. "Approximately ten battle droids led by General Grievous. They're heading toward the gorge."

"Excellent work, Eighteen," Vargus replies. "Do not follow. Give me your coordinates and I will bring the squad to meet you."

You double-check the coordinates on your holomap and relay them to Vargus. Then you and 57 hunker down behind the boulder and wait.

"I can't believe we just encountered General Grievous," 57 says. "Our first mission, and we're playing in the big leagues."

You nod. "He's a little spooky, if you ask me. Those yellow eyes. I wonder what kind of monster lies under all that metal."

57 shakes his head. "Eighteen, you have some strange thoughts sometimes."

Your conversation is interrupted by the sound of approaching footsteps. You grab your blaster, ready to fire—but you don't have to. It's Commander Vargus, with the rest of Excelsior Company behind him.

"All right, Eighteen," Vargus says. "Lead us to these droids you saw."

Vargus has given you an important task, and you don't want to fail him. Luckily, the snow-covered terrain means that it's fairly easy to follow the droid tracks. You lead the squad over a hill and down toward the icy gorge. Two snow-covered mountain walls rise up on either side of the narrow passageway. Vargus studies it for a moment.

"If we follow them in, we risk being trapped," he says. "Our best hope is to follow from above. Maybe they can lead us to the lost legion."

Now your commander takes the lead, hiking up the mountainside overlooking the gorge. When you reach the top, you lay down flat and crawl to the edge of the ridge so you won't be spotted.

Grievous and his droids are in the center of the gorge. You do a quick count and realize there are twelve droids, not ten as you had guessed. The droids seem to be walking in circles. Their metal legs move stiffly, and you think they look pretty odd with their long, thin faces. They look too skinny to be dangerous, but each one holds a black blaster in its metal hands. You know the droid weapons have a continuous fire trigger, which means a battle droid attack can be swift and powerful. It would be a mistake to underestimate them.

General Grievous is in the center of them, his yellow eyes glowing from behind a metal, skull-shaped mask. From this angle, you can see that he has four arms made of metal.

One of the droids walks up to Grievous. "No trace of the army, General."

"Impossible!" Grievous replies. "They could not have vanished without a trace."

Next to Commander Vargus, Dom whispers, "Come on, Commander. Let me sock a thermal detonator down there."

"I don't want to attack unless necessary," Vargus says. "They might be our only chance at finding the legion."

Vargus sounds pretty smart to you. Even though the droids look just as clueless as you are, they might know something you don't.

Beside you, 57 crawls forward to get a closer look. He leans on a patch of tightly packed, overhanging snow. The snow breaks off and falls into the gorge below.

Grievous's eyes immediately shoot up to the top of the ridge.

"Clone troopers!" he yells. "Blast them!"

Bam! Bam! Bam! The snow around you erupts in white clouds as the droid blasters assault the top of the ridge. For a moment, you're stunned. You've battled in simulations before, but it's never been this real.

Captain Vargus, Dom, and Splice are already returning fire. Down below, Grievous reaches under his cloak with two of his arms and pulls out two lightsabers. He activates them and they glow with shimmering blue light. Grievous wields them expertly, deflecting each blast from the clone troopers.

The other rookies are slower to react, just like you. You've got to focus. You aim your DC-15 at one of the battle droids and he's aiming at you at the same time.

Zap! You release the trigger and roll out of the way, the droid's laser narrowly missing you. Then you quickly look down to see if you've hit your target. You're happy to see the droid you hit is facedown in a pile of snow.

In the time it took you to take down one droid, Vargus and the more experienced troopers have taken care of the whole squad. You see Grievous fleeing the gorge, his black cape flying behind him. The gorge is littered with the broken metal bodies of droids.

"So much for following them," Vargus says, standing up. "Let's get down there and see if we can learn anything useful."

You hold your DC-15 in front of you, ready to fire in case another droid squad appears—or if Grievous returns. Then you hike back down the mountainside and enter the gorge.

"Fan out," Vargus orders. "Comb the gorge. I want to make sure we don't miss anything."

You obey, although you're not sure what you're looking for. The metal droid pieces are all rust colored and stand out in the snow.

Then something catches your eye. It's black, and it's not a droid blaster. It's a small rectangle with a screen and buttons on the side. You pick it up.

"Commander," you call out. "I found something."

Turn to page 132.

Since the shots are coming from above you, you decide moving up the path will only bring you closer to danger.

"Head for the cave!" you say.

The three of you run for it.

Bam! Bam! Bam!

Shots explode in the snow at your feet. Just before you reach the cave you feel something smack into your helmet.

You cry out in surprise and make a rolling dive into the cave. The back of your head hurts—but whatever hit you didn't penetrate your armor. Outside the cave, you see a small metal ball burning a hole in the snow.

"They're using slugthrowers," you realize. "They must be Talid. Droids don't normally use such primitive weapons."

"I thought you said the Talid weren't dangerous," 44 says.

"That's what I thought," you reply. "But I know they can be protective of the junk they stockpile. We might be near a cache. They must have snipers protecting it."

"Snipers?" 44 says.

"Our blasters are a lot more powerful than those slugthrowers," you assure him. "We should be able to take them down."

"How?" 57 asks. "We can't even see them."

You know he's right. But you can fix that.

"I'll draw them out," you say. "Pay attention to where the shots are coming from."

You can't decide whether you're brave or foolish. Knowing the slugshot can't penetrate your armor gives you some confidence—although it does hurt. You take a deep breath. Then you jump out of the cave, firing your blaster.

"Hey, Talid! Come and get me!"

The snipers take the bait. You see two figures rise up from the mountainside across the pass. You take a few steps back as 57 and 44 jump forward, blasters blazing.

The aim of both the troopers is dead-on, and you understand why they might have been chosen for the mission—even 44. Both snipers go down.

"Nice work," you tell your men.

You activate the comlink built into your helmet. That was a close call. You need to tell Commander Vargus what happened.

"Commander, Sergeant Eighteen reporting," you say. But there's no response—only static.

"My comlink's down," you tell the others.

57 and 44 both try to contact Vargus.

"Mine, too," 57 says.

"I can't get a signal either," says 44.

"Must be a technical problem," you reason.

"So what now?" 44 asks.

"We might as well see if we can find Falco," you say. "If we got away from those snipers, I'm sure he did, too."

First, you have to make sure there are no more snipers out there. You look outside the cave.

"I'm going to run to that next crevice over there," you say. "Cover me."

You crouch down and run, your blaster ready to fire. You wait for the sound of sniper shots, but none come.

"All clear," you say.

55 and 44 meet up with you.

"I think we can move on," you say. Your squad members nod, and the three of you continue on through the mountain pass. There are no more shots from the mountain—you've taken care of the snipers.

The pass opens up onto a snowy plain. Falco's guess was right—it looks like it could be the enemy base. It's dotted with long, low metal buildings, the kind you find in a makeshift camp.

It's eerily quiet. You are about to call out for Falco,

but think better of it. This could be some kind of trap. You're better off keeping quiet until you know what you're dealing with.

"Let's check the buildings," you say. "Falco might be inside one of them."

You lead the troopers into the compound. Before you enter the first building you notice a strange machine in the center. You move forward to get a closer look.

Suddenly, a figure in fur robes races in front of the machine. You're not sure, but it could be another Talid.

If you fire on the figure, turn to page 153.
If you hold your fire, turn to page 113.

Vargus approaches and takes the object from you. "Appears to be a scanner of some kind," he says. He presses one of the buttons. "Looks like Grievous picked up the record of an energy surge about a kilometer from here. That must be where they were headed."

The commander seems pleased. "This could be the location of the Confederacy's outpost. General Bandis was getting ready to attack there before the legion vanished. I want you and Five-Seven to head to these coordinates. We'll be close behind you. Report if you see anything."

"Yes, sir," you say.

You and 57 head out through the gorge. It opens out into an expanse of white hills. The high-traction soles of your armored boots keep you from slipping as you climb up the first hill.

When you reach the top of the hill, you stop and look around. It's hard to believe. This morning, you woke up in your bunk on Kamino. Now you're on the edges of the galaxy, on a whole new planet.

"You okay?" 57 asks.

"Sure," you say, breaking out of your daydream. "Let's keep moving."

You scale down the hill, trying not to slide, and climb up the next one. Now you can see a small compound of buildings in the distance. You contact Vargus. First you give him your coordinates.

"I can see four buildings approximately five hundred meters ahead," you say. "No sign of inhabitants from here."

"Approach cautiously," Vargus warns. "Don't let 'em see you coming."

You end the transmission and continue your path toward the buildings. The compound is out in the open—there's not much cover around. Then you spot some kind of transport vehicle near the buildings, covered with snow. It's your best hope. You and 57 run from the last hill and dive behind the vehicle, hoping you haven't been seen.

You crouch down, cautiously peering from the side of the transport. Suddenly, a figure darts out from behind one of the buildings. It's tall, and appears to be wearing some kind of metal armor combined with brown robes and thick, black gloves. It's moving fast.

"Come on!" 57 urges. "Let's catch him before he gets away!"

You hesitate for a split second. That seems like the logical thing to do. You and 57 should be able to take down one guy.

But what if there are more of them in there?

If you chase down the armored figure, turn to page 86.

If you hold back and report to Commander Vargus, turn to page 115.

You really want to battle alongside Commander Cody. But a Jedi general just asked you if you want to lead a mission—and you just can't say no.

"I'll lead the attack on the comm station," you say.

"Excellent, sergeant," Obi-Wan Kenobi replies. "Work as quickly as you can. I will mobilize General Bandis and his troops."

You turn to Dom and Falco. "Let's move."

The troopers follow you down the side of the cliff. Dirt kicks up under your boots as you skid down.

You can see that there are a few scattered skirmishes around the comm station. You take cover behind a large boulder and study your surroundings. The station is surrounded by a crude fence. Battle droids are lined up along the perimeter of the fence. There's an unusual-looking tank rolling back and forth in front of the troops. It almost looks like an IG-227 *Hailfire* droid tank. The cockpit of the tank is a round ball of metal topped with an array of gun turrets. Metal rods connect the cockpit to two hooplike wheels.

You've studied droid weaponry extensively. You know the unusual wheels were designed to operate on all kinds of terrain with impressive speed. But a normal *Hailfire* is self-aware—there's no operator in the cockpit. The tank itself is a droid.

This one seems to have been modified. There's a window in the cockpit, and you can see two battle droids inside. They're operating the tank just the way a clone trooper would man a Republic tank.

"Can I blow the place up?" Bruiser asks.

"Of course," you say. "But I think we're going to need to get closer. Falco, can you recon the perimeter and see if there's a way in?"

"Yes, sir," Falco says. He races off and returns a few minutes later.

"Same thing all around," Falco reports. "Droids guarding every inch of that fence. We could storm them and blast our way inside."

"We could," you agree. "If it weren't for that tank. Our armor can't stand up to those guns."

"So we'll risk it," Bruiser says. "We've got to get this done."

You know Bruiser's right. It just seems so dangerous. You almost wish you had let General Kenobi lead the mission instead. What would he do right now?, you wonder.

He'd tear that tank in half with his lightsaber, you realize. But that's not an option for you. If it weren't for that tank . . .

"Wait," you say. "What if we commandeer the tank?

Then we can storm our way inside. Nobody could stop us then."

"So what do we do? Walk up and knock on the window?" Bruiser asks. "See if the droids will let us hitch a ride?"

"I was thinking we could try to reprogram some of those droids over there," you say, nodding to some sleepy-looking guard droids leaning against a guard station a few meters away.

"I like your plan, but reprogramming droids can be tricky," Falco says. "Why don't we launch a surprise attack on the tank? It should be easy to pull those two droid pilots out of there."

Falco's plan sounds risky, but he does have more experience than you. You're not sure what to do.

If you decide to reprogram the guard droids, turn to page 53.

If you take Falco's advice and storm the tank, turn to page 143.

You decide to play it safe.

"I think I'd hinder the operation, sir," you say, nodding to your leg.

"Fine," Vargus says. "All right. Dom, you and Splice take Five-Seven and Three-Six with you."

You all head outside. Dom keeps his blaster pointed at Vylagos. The Skakoan walks up to the machine. It's about the size of a starfighter and looks like a giant engine of some kind, a mass of curved metal tubes and wires. Vylagos fusses over it like a worried mother.

"Such an intricate device," he says, muttering. "Mindless soldiers. No respect for technology."

"Just curious," Vargus says. "The last time this machine went off it sent thousands of soldiers warping through space. Won't it take all of us this time, too?"

"I told you, the machine was activated *accidentally*," Vylagos replies, annoyed. "It's very precise when properly operated. Now then, let's get your squad in position."

Vylagos lines up the four troopers in front of the machine. For a second, you wonder if you made the right decision. Your leg isn't feeling all that bad. You think of all those hours you spent on Kamino, dreaming of exploring the universe. Now you have a chance to do something few other clones will get the chance to do. Are you making a mistake?

But it's too late to change your mind. Vylagos presses a button, and the machine comes to life.

A loud hum fills the air, and soon your whole body feels like it's vibrating. The space around the four troopers starts to ripple like an ocean wave. Then, incredibly, the space compresses, and you watch them all vanish.

BOOM!

You duck for cover as the machine explodes in a cloud of light and smoke. The blast sends Vylagos flying backward.

"Was that supposed to happen?" Vargus asks.

Vylagos slowly gets to his feet. "The machine must have been damaged when it was activated the first time," he says.

"So what happened to my men? Did they transport?" Vargus asks.

"It is possible," Vylagos says. "There is no way of knowing now. And no way to bring them back."

"Yes there is," Vargus says grimly. "You're working for the Republic now. You're going to build us a new machine."

"But that will take months!" the Skakoan protests.

"I don't care how long it takes," Vargus says. "Just make it happen."

Your commander nods at you. "Eighteen, meet your new best friend. I don't want you to leave his side until our men are back. Got that?"

"Yes, sir," you reply.

A cold chill comes over you as you realize what has happened. It looks like you were smart to stay behind after all. Sure, babysitting Vylagos isn't going to be fun, but it's better than vanishing into oblivion. You just hope that wherever the rest of your squad is, they'll be all right until you can find them.

THE END

"Let's try the gorge," Falco says.

You follow the ARF down the trail into the mountain gorge. Steep mountain cliffs rise up on either side of you. You don't feel the piercing wind down here, and the mountain walls buffer you from the blinding snow.

Falco pauses at the opening of the gorge and scans it with the macrobinoculars built into his helmet.

"Looks like we made a good choice," he says. "I can see a small compound of buildings on the other end. Could be the outpost we're looking for."

You start to feel hopeful for the first time since you stepped off of the ship. You trek behind Falco as he leads you through the gorge.

Suddenly, you see Falco fall in front of you, and realize you're falling, too. The ground beneath your feet is breaking away. You brace yourself for the landing.

Thud! You slam into hard frozen earth. It knocks the wind out of you. Groaning, you sit up. Falco is standing next to you.

You hear the sound of creaking metal and look up. A rack of metal bars slides overhead, trapping you and Falco in this hole in the ground.

"What's going on?" you wonder.

"Looks like we're in some kind of animal trap," Falco replies. "There's a big hairy snow beast on this planet, something like a wampa beast. It's a major food source for the Talid people who live on Ando Prime."

"So if it's an animal trap, we should be able to get out of it, right?" you ask hopefully.

"Not so sure about that," Falco says. "The walls are pretty smooth, and we don't have a grappling hook. We'll have to wait until someone finds us."

"Like a search party?" you ask.

"Or the Talid," Falco says matter-of-factly.

You let this sink in. You wonder what will happen if the Talid find you first. You just hope that wampa beast is the only meat they like to eat.

THE END

Falco's plan might be more dangerous, but it's faster—and will probably be more successful.

"You're right," you tell Falco. "Let's wait until the tank is rolling away from us. We'll storm from behind."

You crouch down and peer out from behind the rock. The droids seem to be making a fixed pattern, rolling across the fence in one direction and then the other. You wait until the droid turns and rolls away from you.

"Move out!" you hiss.

You're fast, and you reach the tank first. You somersault under the cockpit, then swing yourself on top of it.

The droid pilots are too surprised to react. They frantically fire the turrets, but the guns are pointing away from you.

BAM! You shatter the cockpit hull with your blaster. You grab one of the droids by the neck and toss him onto the ground.

Falco's beside you now, and he tosses out the other droid. Then he pulls Bruiser up into the cockpit with you.

"Let's crash this party!" Bruiser says.

Falco operates the turrets as you pilot the tank.

You spin it around and zoom toward the fence. It easily crushes under the weight of your wheels. Once you're inside, Bruiser hurls two pulse grenades into the comm station.

"Let's roll!" Bruiser yells.

You race out of the comm station. The bulky tank doesn't go very fast. For a second, you wonder if you will get away in time.

BOOM!

Broken pieces of the comm center clatter against the sides of the tank, but you and Falco and Bruiser are safe inside. You look behind to see that the entire station is a smoking pile of rubble. You've done it!

You report to Commander Cody. He laughs when he sees you all in the tank.

"What are you waiting for?" he asks. "Go blast some droids with that baby!"

You join the battle. Falco takes down rows of surprised droids with the tank's cannons. Bruiser gleefully tosses out pulse grenades, wiping out scores of droids with each throw.

With General Kenobi and Commander Cody in the field, the rest of the operation goes smoothly. A few hours later you're back on the ship, hanging out in the troopers' quarters. 57 and 44 want to hear every detail of your adventure.

"You should have seen your sergeant commandeer that droid tank," Bruiser tells them. "He was a real ace out there."

"Yeah, Ace," Falco says. "Nice job."

You freeze.

Falco just called you Ace. You finally have your nickname! And it's not a bad one, either.

Now if you can only figure out how to dye your crew cut bright red . . .

THE END

"We were all transported to this place in the middle of battle," General Bandis explains. "That battle has never stopped. I just received intelligence that the droids are activating a machine capable of destroying half the legion in one strike. Another invention of that wretched scientist."

"So you've meet Vylagos," Falco says.

"Skakoans will do anything for money," he says. "But I'm afraid by the time I gather the legion together for transport it will be too late. I need to send a unit to destroy that machine."

"We'll go," Falco says.

General Bandis nods. "My troops have been battling for days."

He gives Falco a small holoprojector. A schematic of the droid base camp appears in the air in front of him.

"None of the large buildings in the outpost transported with us," General Bandis tells you. "The machine is out in the open, but it is surrounded by droid tanks. It won't be easy getting past."

"We'll find a way," Falco promises.

Falco leads you, Splice, and 44 to the droid camp. The intelligence General Bandis got was right. A line of Corporate Alliance NR-N99 *Persuader* tank droids surrounds the perimeter of the camp. Behind them, you can see marching troops of droids.

"There's got to be a way in," Falco says.

If you and the squad go left around the perimeter, turn to page 26.

If you and the squad head right around the perimeter, turn to page 51.

"Do what you need to do," Falco tells you. "I'm going out to search the rest of the buildings."

He leaves, and you're alone with the Skakoan and the small FX-3 medical droid. You reach into your bag and prepare a bacta injection. Then you take a deep breath and plunge it into the Skakoan's abdomen.

The Skakoan is still. Then he sits up with a start.

"Where am I?" he asks. He speaks in a strange accent, and his voice is projected through a small speaker at the mouth of his face mask.

"Ando Prime," you say. "On an outpost of the Separatist Army."

"Yes, yes, of course," the Skakoan says. He quickly shuts the armor over his abdomen.

Falco enters. "Commander Vargus and the squad are on the way. There's some kind of strange machine out there." He aims his blaster at the Skakoan. "What's his status?"

"I am Vylagos," the Skakoan replies. "I am a scientist—an engineer."

"An engineer for the Confederacy?" Falco asks.

"In a manner, yes," Vylagos replies. "I am under their employ. Or rather, I *was* under their employ."

"Can you tell us what happened to the droid army

and the Republic's legion?" you ask. "We keep hearing they vanished into thin air, but that doesn't make sense."

"I'd be happy to tell you," Vylagos replies. "For a price."

Falco moves one step closer, his blaster pointed directly at Vylagos. The scientist seems to understand.

"Well, yes," he says, coughing a little. "It's quite simple, actually. The Separatists hired me to create a hyperspace warping device. I have been working here on Ando Prime under the protection of General Terrus. Then your Republic legion attacked, and the device was accidentally activated."

"What's a hyperspace warping device, and what happens when it's activated?" you ask.

"My device was designed to create controlled rifts in hyperspace in order to instantly warp large numbers of droid units across the galaxy," Vylagos tells you. "I believe the Separatists were planning to launch a surprise attack on Coruscant."

"So the legion—and the droid army—got transported somewhere?" Falco asks. "Where are they?"

"I am not completely sure," Vylagos replies. "The machine was not programmed for Coruscant when it was activated. The troops appear to have been sent to a planet beyond the Outer Rim. I was fortunate enough to be off the base when the accident happened. I returned to examine the machine, but there was a small malfunction, and I was injured."

Falco shakes his head. "Wait until Vargus hears this."

Commander Vargus and the rest of the squad arrive a short while later. Vylagos repeats his story. He tells the commander that he can repair the machine. The scientist claims he can bring the lost legion back—if a small squad is sent to their location first with a retrieval device, a sort of homing beacon. Vylagos can use the beacon to hone in on the legion and warp them back to Ando Prime.

"Then that's what we'll do," Vargus says. "Falco, I want you and Dom to lead a unit to the other side. Take Eighteen here and Five-Seven with you."

You're not sure whether to be excited or afraid. If Vylagos fixes the machine, you're going to be transported way out beyond the Outer Rim! There's no guarantee that you'll make it—and you have no clue what you'll find when you get there.

But you're a clone, and clones go wherever duty takes them. You decide to focus on the exciting part. You're about to go where few clones have gone before— well, except for the five thousand in the 313th Legion.

You make camp at the base. Vylagos works through the night, fixing the machine. The next morning, it's time to embark on your mission. Vylagos lines you up in front of the machine.

"Don't move," he warns. Behind him, Vargus grins.

"See you soon," he says.

You hope he's right. The scientist presses a button, and you suddenly feel a strong pull on your body. You want to scream, but before you can, the space around you suddenly blinks.

You're not on Ando Prime anymore. You feel two strong arms grab you from behind. You turn your head to see that two clone troopers have a hold on you!

"We're taking you to General Bandis," one of the clones says.

The rest of your squad has made it here safely, too—although you're not sure where *here* is. The planet's surface is rocky and barren, and you're not cold anymore. The troopers lead you to a command station, and a Jedi in a brown tunic rushes toward you. He has dark brown skin and four small horns on his forehead. His lightsaber handle hangs from a belt around his waist.

"General Bandis, these troopers came through the hyperspace warp," says the trooper holding you.

"If they got here, I assume they know the way back," the Jedi replies.

"We do," Falco says. "We've brought a homing

beacon with us. We need to gather the legion and activate it."

General Bandis is thoughtful. "My legion is scattered, battling the droid army," he says. "We're close to victory. Can you help us finish this up so I can make sure all of my men get back safely?"

You can't believe your luck. You're about to fight some droids—side by side with a Jedi general!

Turn to page 67.

It could be another Talid sniper.

"Open fire!" you yell.

The air explodes in plasma fire, but the figure is fast. He darts out of the way, and you hit the machine behind him instead.

A loud hum fills the air. You start to feel strange. Something is up with that machine.

"Run!" you yell.

But it's too late. You feel a strong pull on your body so intense you want to scream. Then it stops as quickly as it started.

You're not on Ando Prime anymore. You're on a battlefield on a red, rocky planet. Thousands of clones and droids are battling around you.

You have a feeling you've found the lost legion— but you have no idea where you are, or how to get back to Ando Prime.

THE END

Trying to set charges in four different places seems too risky. You're pretty sure targeting the reactor will work. You tell Falco your plan.

"Good thinking," he agrees. "It's not far from here. We just need to go down one level."

He goes to the doorway and looks both ways. "There's an elevator that leads down to the power center. We'll have to circumvent the cameras."

You follow Falco to the elevator. He opens the door and quickly zaps the camera inside with his blaster.

"That's one way to do it," he quips.

The elevator takes you to the sub-basement. The door opens, and Falco slides outside, motioning for you to be quiet.

The lithium reactor is guarded by two battle droids. They're arguing, just like the first two droids you spotted.

"Bet I can," one droid is saying.

"Bet you can't," says the other.

"Can too," says the first droid. He bends over backward so that his head touches the floor. "See?"

The other droid shakes his head. "You must have a screw loose," he says.

Zap! Falco takes down the droid with his DC-15

blaster, then nods to you. You take the cue and aim your plasma gun at the first droid.

"Hey! Wait!" the droid cries. He tries to stand up, but he can't get back into position.

Zap! You aim and hit your target. Now the way is clear.

"Set that charge and let's get out of here," Falco says.

You move quickly, nestling five detonators by the reactor's core. This isn't a tunnel—you want the biggest bang you can get.

"Charges set. We're heading to the surface, Commander," Falco reports over the comlink.

Vargus gives Falco the squad's coordinates. The ARF knows a quick way to the surface, and you escape without getting caught. You meet the squad on a nearby hill overlooking the factory. Vargus is happy to see you.

"All right," he tells you. "Let's see what you can do."

You hold up the detonator and press the button. Then you wait.

KA-BOOM!

The factory explodes in the center first, a huge explosion of blue light and fire. The ground shakes underneath you. Sparks of blue light shoot out, landing just meters in front of you. They sizzle as they land in the snow.

Then the blast ripples out to the ends of the factory,

and you watch as it collapses in on itself. You can't believe it. The factory must have taken thousands of hours to build. But you've taken it down in mere minutes. You knew blowing stuff up would be fun, but the awesome power of it hits you for a minute.

"Nice work, rookie," Vargus says, and once again you feel proud. You want to say thanks, but you can't even speak. You're still a little dazed by everything that's happened.

Vargus turns and motions to the other side of the hill. "This day's just getting better and better. Looks like we found the Separatist outpost."

You follow his gaze and see buildings scattered below, brown boxes on a snowy landscape. Vargus sends Falco down first to investigate. You wait until he reports back.

"All buildings clear," he says. "But there's something here you've just gotta see."

You head down to the outpost and meet Falco in front of a strange machine. It looks like some kind of large engine. Curved tubes snake in and out of it. You don't remember seeing a picture of it in any of your studies on Kamino. The machine is being guarded by an electromagnetic field generator.

"I need you to deactivate the EMF," Vargus tells you. "Something tells me that machine is the key to what happened to the lost legion."

Deactivating the generator is a little different than blowing stuff up. You wonder what the best approach is.

If you set off an electric charge to fry the EMF signal, turn to page 44.

If you decide to blow up the EMF device, turn to page 55.

You didn't come this far to stay behind. Vylagos might be lying—but you're a clone trooper. You've been trained to get into dangerous situations, and that's what you're going to do.

"Leg's fine," you say. You hop off the table to prove it.

"Good," Vargus says. "I need you and Five-Seven to go with Splice and Dom and get that legion back here."

You all go outside and watch while Vylagos fusses over the machine. It looks almost like a large engine made up of connecting curved tubes. Vylagos starts pressing buttons, and the tubes begin to glow.

"When the machine was accidentally activated, the hyperdrive warp sucked in everyone within a two-hundred meter radius," he says. "I can program it to be quite specific, so only your squad members will go through. I will keep the wormhole open. Once there, they will need to bring your lost legion to the wormhole's coordinates as quickly as possible. I am not sure how long I can keep it open. The machine is still in the testing stage."

"Don't worry," Dom says confidently. "We'll get 'em back fast."

"In one piece if we're lucky," Splice adds.

Vylagos orders the four of you to stand together. He starts the machine, and a loud hum fills the air. You're not sure what to expect, and you suddenly wonder if being warped across the galaxy is going to hurt.

A loud buzzing sound fills your ears. Your whole body starts to vibrate.

WHOOSH!

It feels like all of the oxygen is sucked out of you for a second. Then the feeling stops. You look around and see Dom, Splice, and 57 around you.

You've made it.

As you regain your bearings, you realize you're in the middle of a military camp on a rocky, barren planet. There must be thousands of clone troopers around you. Then a man in a brown tunic rushes up to you. His skin is dark brown, and four small horns are growing from the top of his head.

"General Bandis!" Dom says.

"I hope I'm not seeing things," the Jedi general says. "Did you four just transport here out of nowhere?"

"Yes, sir," Splice replies. "We've been sent to take the legion back to Ando Prime. The machine that sent you here is operational."

"That's good news," General Bandis says. "Can you help me? We've got to get five thousand men back through that wormhole."

You and your squadmates help General Bandis round up the legion. Vylagos is true to his word, and soon the 313th Legion is safely back on Ando Prime—and so are you.

"And what of the droid army?" Vylagos asks.

"Guess they've got a new planet to call home," Commander Vargus says. He turns to Dom. "Be my guest."

Dom grins—and throws a thermal detonator into the machine.

THE END